The Lineman

Also by Tom Milton

The Last Resort

The Godmother

Eden Valley

The Silver Locket

Orphans of War

Invisible Wounds

Leave of Absence

Outside the Gate

The Golden Door

Sara's Laughter

A Shower of Roses

Infamy

All the Flowers

The Admiral's Daughter

No Way to Peace

The Lineman

Tom Milton

NEPPERHAN PRESS, LLC
YONKERS, NY

Published by Nepperhan Press, LLC
P.O. Box 1448, Yonkers, NY 10702
nepperhan@optonline.net
nepperhan.com

PUBLISHER'S NOTE
This is a work of fiction. Names, characters, places, and incidents
are the product of the author's imagination or are used fictitiously,
and any resemblance to actual persons, living or dead, events, or
locales is entirely coincidental.

Printed in the United States of America

Library of Congress Control Number: 2019944381

ISBN 978-1-7320634-4-0

Cover art was licensed from Publitek, Inc.

For Marie

And I need you more than want you,
and I want you for all time,
and the Wichita Lineman is still on the line.
    Jimmy Webb, "Wichita Lineman"

A habit is hell for those you love.
    Billie Holiday, "Lady Sings the Blues"

Yonkers, 2016

ONE

BEFORE SHE GOT into the panel truck Paola stood and gazed at the house they had bought almost eighteen years ago. At that time it needed work, which was why they could afford it, and over the years they had improved it to its present condition, which was why they could sell it for what they needed. It was empty now, with the last load of Briana's clothes packed in the truck, and it was ready to be occupied by a new family.

Taking a last look at the house, Paola felt the compounding effect of its loss, and she had trouble fighting back tears, especially remembering the happy day when she and Danny arrived here ahead of the moving van, with Briana still safely inside of her getting ready to be born. They were going to have their own house and start their own family. They had no idea what would happen to them, and now she felt sympathy for the girl she had been and even for the boy Danny had been.

As she reached to open the door of the truck she noticed that "Borgatti Electric" had been defaced, maliciously scraped by a tool or a knife. She assumed it was a random act of vandalism because she couldn't think of anyone who might have a vendetta against her family. Though the damage was minor, it felt like salt in an open wound, and she winced with pain as she climbed into the driver's seat.

She started the engine and moved out into the street. It led to Roberts Avenue, where she turned right, heading downhill toward the river. She was taking the load to her parents' house, which was less than a half mile away. It was a two-family house, which her parents had shared with her grandparents until about five years ago when her grandmother passed away. At that time her parents moved from the second floor to the first floor, and they rented the second floor until two months ago when Paola needed a place to live. She was living there now, on the same floor where she and her brothers had grown up. Briana was nominally living there too, but she hadn't been there for several days. She was staying with her father, refusing even to help move her own clothes. It was as if she believed that as long as her clothes remained in that house it was still possible for them to live there as a united family.

Paola turned left on Park Avenue and at the end of Kinsley Park she arrived at Morsemere Avenue, where she turned left and went a little farther, luckily finding a parking place across the street from her parents' house. The driveway was taken by her father's car and her car, and the truck was normally parked at the office on Nepperhan Avenue, so she would have to take it there when she was done using it. Since she didn't expect Briana to return that day, she would have to get her father to drive his car to the office and bring her back. For a while she sat there with her hands on the steering wheel and blamed Briana for not helping to move her own clothes from their old home to their new one. She also blamed Danny for not making Briana help her. But for some reason, which made no sense, she blamed herself for their behavior.

She got out and went to the back of the truck and opened the doors. The last thing she put in was a bag of dirty clothes, so it was the first thing she took out. She also took a pile of evidently clean clothes and, together with the bag, carried them to the front door, which her father opened for her just in time.

"You got no one helping you?" he said, looking beyond her toward the truck.

"I don't need anyone," she said, deflecting his comment.

"Is it just clothes?" he asked as she passed by him into the hallway.

"Yeah, it's just clothes." Briana had already taken her phone and her computer, along with their respective chargers, to Danny's apartment.

"Then I can help you," her father said, going out the door.

"You really don't have to," Paola told him. "I can handle it."

"Yeah, I know. You can handle everything."

She knew he didn't mean this sardonically, he meant she took upon herself more than any human being could handle, and she should let other people help her. She had heard this before not only from him but also from teachers, coaches, and bosses, and she acknowledged some truth in it, so she didn't argue, she let him help her carry Briana's clothes from the truck to the hallway, where after making a pile of them she started carrying them up the stairs. She drew the line at his helping her with that.

Except for the bag of dirty clothes she deposited everything on Briana's bed. With her father's comment fresh in her ears, she resisted the compulsion to take the dirty clothes down to the basement and put them into the washing machine. Since the age of fourteen Briana had been responsible for doing her own laundry, and now that she was seventeen it wasn't a time to let her regress in this respect, especially when she was regressing in other respects. If the girl wasn't willing to do her own laundry she would have to accept the consequences.

Physically and emotionally drained, Paola got a bottle of white wine out of the refrigerator, poured a glass, and sat down at the table where she and Danny and Briana had eaten so many meals together. With her eyes on the clock over the sink, she replayed the scene in which she explained to her parents what was happening with her and Danny.

"You're getting a divorce?" her father asked, dumbfounded. They were sitting in the living room, with her parents in the easy chairs and her on the sofa. She had come to tell them as soon as she and Danny signed the papers.

"It's not a divorce," she patiently explained again. "It's a legal separation."

"What's the difference?"

"If you get a divorce, it ends the marriage. If you get a legal separation, it doesn't end the marriage, but you're no longer legally responsible for each other."

"Do you live together?" her mother asked.

"No, you have to live separately, or else the agreement isn't valid. But you stay married."

"You live separately but you stay married?" her father said. "That makes no sense. If you live separately, you're not really married."

"Yeah, we are. We're legally married."

Her father shook his head, saying: "This sounds like it was concocted by a smartass lawyer. What's the point?"

"The point is to prevent Danny from ruining us financially. If we're legally separated, then I'm not liable for his debts."

"So you want to stay married to Danny," her mother said, "but you don't want to be liable for his debts."

"That's the purpose of the arrangement."

"Why do you want to stay married to him?" her father asked.

"I still love him. And I took a vow when I married him," Paola added. "For better or for worse, for richer or for poorer, in sickness and in health."

Her father was silent for a while, and then he said: "If you're still legally married to him, does he still own half of the business?"

"No. He gets half of the profits, but he doesn't own any of the business."

"How did he get that bank loan?" her mother asked.

"I told you. He went to them and asked for it."

"You both didn't have to sign for it?" her father asked.

"No. Either of us could sign for a loan."

Her father frowned. "Well, your brother shouldn't have written the agreement that way."

"Don't blame Anthony. I asked him to write the agreement that way. I wanted Danny and me to be equal partners in the business."

"But under the new agreement you're not equal partners."

"No, we're not," she said. "Danny doesn't have the power to borrow money."

"If he tries to get a loan, will a bank know he doesn't have the power to borrow money?"

"A bank will want to see our documents, which will show that he doesn't have the power to borrow money."

Her father took a long deep breath and exhaled in a sigh. "Well, if he gets into debt some other way, will this arrangement protect you?"

"It will if we fulfill the condition of living separately."

"What if you—?" her father stopped as if he was embarrassed to say it.

"You mean what if I spent a night with him?"

Her father nodded, avoiding the look her mother gave him.

"That's not likely," she hastily assured him. "At least not in our present situation."

Her father still had a question. "Will you get enough money from selling your house to pay off the loan?"

"I'll get enough, but I won't have anything left of our savings."

"And you really want to live with us?" her mother asked.

"I do," she said honestly. She needed her family, and she wasn't going to pretend that she didn't. She was past the stage where she had to prove her independence.

"You don't have to pay us rent," her father offered.

"I'll pay whatever rent you could get in the market. I can pay you rent and support Briana and help Danny. But I can't do more."

"Why do you have to help Danny after what he did to you?" her mother asked.

"I have to help him because he can't live on what he gets for disability."

"He could get a job," her father said.

"I know he could, and I keep hoping he'll get a job. But in the meantime I don't want him to end up homeless."

"He won't end up homeless."

She really didn't believe he would. But something else might happen, so it wasn't only financial ruin that she wanted to protect her family from, it was something that she didn't want her parents to know about.

Sipping the wine, she acknowledged that she hadn't told her parents the whole truth. She had told them about Danny's addictions to opioids and video games and gambling. She had told them he ran up an enormous debt from gambling and without her knowledge took a bank loan to pay it off, using his power as a partner in the business. She had told them the business couldn't repay the bank loan, so they had to sell their house to repay it. She had told them she decided it was better to lose their house, which represented all their savings over eighteen years, than to lose the business, which represented all her father's hard work over a lifetime. But she hadn't told them Danny's debt was to the mob.

Her thoughts were interrupted by the sound of the intercom, which her parents had installed while they were living on the second floor and their parents, by then elderly, were living on the first floor. They had removed the intercom while they were living on the first floor and renting the second floor to people outside the family, but now it was back, and it was easier than using the phone to communicate between the floors. Unlike a phone, which usually had a marketing robot at the other end when you answered it, the intercom was accessible only to the family, so when it sounded you knew it was family.

The intercom was on the counter, to the right of the sink, so Paola had to get up and walk over there. She pressed the button and said: "Mom?"

"It's me," her father said. "You want to take the truck back now?"

"Oh, yeah. I'll be right down."

At least that would give her something to do for the next half hour or so, instead of sitting at the kitchen table, drinking wine and feeling sad.

Her father was already outside, standing by his car. It was a Ford, as was the truck. He would buy only American cars, and he trusted Fords as if there was a family connection between him and the company.

"I'll follow you," he told her.

"Okay," she said, going to the truck.

She led the way down Morsemere Avenue with her father behind her. She was conscious of being his only hope for the future of the family business. Her older brothers had declined his offers to participate in the business, and they pursued more lucrative professions, with Dominic becoming an accountant and

Anthony becoming a lawyer. While her father was proud to have an accountant and a lawyer in the family, at the same time he was disappointed in his boys for not wanting to succeed him as owners and managers of Borgatti Electric. And it had been very hard for him to accept a girl as his successor.

Her opening had come on the day when fathers were supposed to take their daughters to work and show them what they did outside the home. Her father resisted the idea, but her mother supported it, no doubt being confident that Paola wouldn't like the work her father did. But her mother should have known better because Paola always wanted to do what her brothers did, and being a girl, she was excluded from their activities except for sports, at which she was just as good as a boy. Without any competition from her brothers for the goal of becoming an electrician, she advanced in stages, taking classes, accumulating the necessary years of experience, passing the examinations, and finally getting her license.

She turned left on Frederic Place and then rounded the block to Montague Street, where she turned right and headed down to Nepperhan Avenue. Her father was still behind her, keeping at least three car lengths between them. In teaching her to drive, her father always emphasized the importance of keeping a safe distance between your car and the car ahead of you. But she didn't really learn that lesson until the time on a snowy day when she followed a car too closely and skidded into it, damaging her radiator.

On Nepperhan she turned left and came to the two-story brick building that her father had acquired when she was a girl. It had room for offices and equipment, and in the back was a parking area large enough to accommodate eight trucks. She drove her truck around the building and into the only available space. The other spaces were occupied by trucks of the same model, the same year, which her father had bought on a fleet discount.

Her father pulled up behind her and waited while she locked the truck. She kept the keys, which she could return to the office on Monday.

She got into her father's car, and they drove away with the sound of Tony Bennett on the radio. She welcomed the sound because it relieved her of the pressure to talk, though with her father she didn't feel much pressure.

They were climbing the hill on Montague when her father broke their silence, asking: "Did you get all your things out of the house?"

"Yeah. The last load was Briana's clothes."

"From what I saw, she didn't help you."

"No, she didn't. She's mad at me."

"She blames you for splitting with her father?"

"Yeah. And she's right to blame me."

"No, she's not. It's not your fault what happened to Danny."

"I know, but I feel like it *is* my fault. Is that crazy?"

"Yeah, it's crazy. What happened to Danny he did to himself, and we all know it."

"We all know it except Danny," she murmured. "And except Briana."

She parted with her father in the hallway and climbed the stairs. She was wondering if she should contact Briana, sending her a text message and asking where she was. She didn't want her daughter spending time with Danny, who stayed up all night on his computer and slept all day. Briana had picked up his habits, which were hard to break. If she tried to get Briana out of bed before noon on a weekend she met resistance, and she stood by helpless while Briana decamped to her father's apartment, where she could do what he did—nothing.

Briana was about to start her senior year in high school when Paola learned about Danny's gambling. With very good grades and very good test scores, Briana was qualified to enter the nursing program at St. Catherine and pursue her dream. Paola tried to shield Briana from the problem, and she even delayed dealing with it, hoping that if Briana started well in her senior year she would be motivated to continue doing well. But the delay only made things worse, and when they finally had to sell their house to repay the loan that Danny had taken to pay his gambling debts, Paola could no longer hide what was happening.

In explaining to Briana why they had to sell their house Paola was careful to avoid blaming Danny, but Briana reacted as if her mother had invented the whole thing as a pretext for splitting with her father, casting her mother as the evil doer and her father as the victim. No amount of evidence could convince Briana otherwise, and she took revenge against her mother by deciding not to do her homework.

As she entered the kitchen Paola spotted the empty wine glass on the table, but she resisted the temptation to refill it, and instead she sat down and texted Briana, asking where she was. She knew that with kids the protocol was to reply promptly to a text message, so she waited, hoping for a reply. But there was no reply.

She was about to get the wine bottle out of the refrigerator when she heard footsteps coming up the stairs with the fatalism of a prisoner mounting the scaffold. The door opened, and there was Briana, looking as if she had spent the night in Kinsley Park.

"Hey, honey," Paola said softly. "Where've you been?"

Briana shrugged as if it didn't matter where she had been. She shuffled across the floor and pulled out a chair and sat down heavily.

"Were you with your father?"

Briana nodded.

"How is he?"

"Not good. He has a lot of pain in his shoulder."

His downfall had begun with his shoulder, which he injured almost five years ago falling out of a cherry picker while working on a utility pole. Whenever he told people what happened they always asked how he could fall out of a cherry picker, whose main purpose was to protect linemen from falling. But he never told them how he had fallen, he only blamed the faulty equipment. "Is he taking anything for it?"

"Yeah. The usual."

The usual was an opioid. "Does it help?"

"A little. But it's awful for him."

Paola didn't comment, though she was disheartened to hear that Danny was taking opioids again. It had been so hard to get him off opioids the first time. "What about you?"

"What do you mean?"

"You look like you spent the night in Kinsley Park."

"I spent the night with Dad. I just didn't take a shower."

"Well, why don't you take a shower and change your clothes."

Briana said nothing, but she slowly got up and headed for her bedroom.

Paola again resisted the temptation to pour herself another glass of wine, being mindful of her husband's addictions. She sat at the table, supposing that Briana must be hungry since all she would have gotten to eat at her father's apartment would be snacks, with an emphasis on chips. He didn't even bother to have Chinese takeout food delivered to him.

She hadn't planned to cook dinner for Briana, whom she hadn't expected home tonight. She thought about taking her to D & V, the neighborhood Italian restaurant down the street, where Briana could get the cheese ravioli that she liked. But then the intercom sounded, and this time it was her mother, inviting her to come down for dinner.

"Briana's here," she told her mother.

"I know. I saw her car on the street." Her mother didn't miss anything that happened on the street. "I'm making lasagna, which I know she likes."

"What time should we come down?"

"As soon as you can. It's almost done."

"Okay. Thanks."

She went to the door of Briana's bedroom, which as usual was closed. She rapped gently, saying: "Briana?"

There was no reply.

"Nonna invited us to dinner. She made lasagna."

"What kind of lasagna?

"I don't know. I assume it's the usual kind."

It took a while for Briana to say: "Okay. But I can't stay long."

"We don't have to stay long," Paola said. "But we do have to eat. And she said to come as soon as we can."

"I'll be out in a minute," Briana said.

It was more than a minute, but when the girl emerged from her bedroom she looked much better. Her hair was clean and she was wearing clean clothes, a tee shirt over jeans, which looked as if they were becoming too tight for her.

They went down the stairs with Paola leading.

The two apartments shared a common hallway, with separate doors, and the door to her parents' apartment was slightly ajar, so they could walk right into the living room, where her father was watching a college football game.

He took his eyes off the television to greet Briana, who stopped to kiss him on the forehead before following Paola into the kitchen. Paola waited at a safe distance while her mother took the pan of lasagna out of the oven and set it on the table. Then. after wiping her hands on her apron, her mother turned to Briana and opened her arms for a hug.

Briana responded positively, having nothing against her grandparents because they never made her do things she didn't want to do.

Paola carried the pan of lasagna into the dining room and set it on the table, which had four places set. With an extra leaf the table could accommodate her brothers, their wives, and their children. They were all there for the usual occasions—Thanksgiving, Christmas Eve, Easter, and the Fourth of July—though this year Danny would probably decline the invitations.

They sat down and her mother said grace and then her father served them from the pan, which he had pulled toward him.

For a while there wasn't much conversation, and then her mother asked Briana: "Are you still working at Starbucks?"

"No," Briana said with food in her mouth.

"Are you working somewhere else?"

"No. I'm looking for a job."

As an act of mercy, Paola let the fib pass. The truth was, Briana had quit her job at Starbucks weeks ago and she still hadn't started looking for another job.

"They're opening a new supermarket on Nepperhan. They might have a position there."

"I don't want a checkout job. It doesn't pay anything."

"It pays more than doing nothing," her father said.

"I can find something better," Briana said.

The focus of their conversation shifted to other members of the family, and after finishing her plate of lasagna Briana pulled out her phone.

"Not at the dinner table," Paola quietly reminded her.

Briana gave her a hostile look but she put away her phone and sat there for a while before asking: "Can I be excused?"

"Have you had enough to eat?" her mother asked.

"Yeah, and it was great. Thank you, Nonna."

Briana got up and left them and headed out the door.

When she was gone her mother asked: "How's she doing?"

"She's not doing well," Paola said. "She's developing some bad habits, which she's picking up from her father."

"Can you keep her away from him?"

"No, I can't. She's allowed to see him."

"You mean your agreement didn't give you full custody?" her father asked.

"It wasn't about custody. That wasn't the issue."

"Well, if he's having a bad influence on her, there must be something you could do."

"My lawyer says I could get a protective order, but I don't want to do that. I think it would make things even worse."

"You need to find something for her to do," her mother said.

"She has her homework to do, and if she did it, that would keep her busy. But she doesn't do it. She doesn't have any motivation."

"Maybe she just needs time to get over what happened."

"That's what I'm hoping," Paola said.

She stayed with her parents for another hour, helping her mother clean up and letting her father bring her up to date on the football season.

Back in her apartment, she found the door to her daughter's bedroom tightly closed. She knew that Briana was lying on her bed, playing a violent game on her laptop or watching a violent movie. She would stay up all night, as her father did, and finally go to sleep when the birds started singing.

By now Paola felt justified in pouring herself another glass of wine. She went into the living room and turned on the television. There was news of yet another mass shooting at a school where eleven children were killed and several others were wounded. It aroused in her a feeling of sympathy for children growing up in a world where you couldn't even go to school without the risk of being killed or maimed. This feeling extended to her daughter, whom she couldn't blame for her behavior. In fact, she finally had to admit that Briana needed help beyond what she as a mother could give her.

She turned off the television and got her phone and called Gabby, her closest friend. They had grown up together in this neighborhood and gone from kindergarten through high school together, graduating from Sacred Heart and then pursuing different careers. While she was working at her father's business, gaining the experience required for her electrician license, Gabby was attending St. Catherine, earning a bachelor's degree in psychology and then a master's in school psychology. After working for several years in the Bronx she got a position in Yonkers, where she counseled high school students. In the meantime she had gotten married and had two girls who were now in middle school. When they were younger Briana used to babysit them.

It was Saturday night, and since there would be a football game that her husband had to watch, Gabby would probably be at home and available to talk.

"Hey, Paola," her friend said, answering the phone.

"Are you in the middle of anything?"

"No. We were only having sex."

Paola laughed, knowing her friend's sense of humor, and already she felt better. "Well, I need your advice about Briana."

"How's she doing?"

"She's not doing well," Paola admitted, conscious of having

answered in the exact same words to her mother's question. "She's in a deep hole."

"You mean depressed?"

"That's one word for it. But I don't think it captures the full sense of what's wrong with her. And whatever it is, she caught it from her father."

"You mean she inherited it from him?"

"She might have, but you knew him before he changed, and he wasn't the way he is now."

"No, he wasn't," Gabby agreed.

"She doesn't want to do anything. She doesn't care about anything. She doesn't even seem to care if she lives or dies."

"You think she's suicidal?"

"No. She doesn't *care* enough to kill herself."

"Wow," Gabby said softly. "I hope you don't feel it's your fault."

"I do feel it's my fault, but this isn't about me. It's about her. And I was hoping you could recommend a therapist."

"A psychologist?"

"Yeah, I don't want her to see a psychiatrist. I think she needs therapy, not drugs."

"Well, there're a lot of therapists in Hastings, I guess because they're in such demand there." Gabby still lived in Yonkers, near Sacred Heart, and she liked taking shots at towns that looked down on Yonkers.

"It has to be a woman."

"I understand. I know one who might be good for her."

"Has she worked with your students?"

"Oh, yeah. I mean, what she does with them is confidential, but I see the results, and those kids are doing better."

"What's her name?"

"Janice Healy. And guess what."

Paola waited.

"She's an ex-nun."

"Really?"

"Really. She was a Sister of the Redemption. In fact, she teaches at St. Catherine, though she wasn't there when I was there."

"Where was she?"

"Doing a ministry in Latin America. I don't remember which country."

"Does she teach psychology?"

"Yeah, she teaches adolescent psychology."

Paola had gone to St. Catherine later than Gabby, getting a degree in business administration, and she had taken the basic course in psychology, but the professor wasn't an ex-nun or even a woman. He was a man who counseled drug addicts. "Is she listed on the internet?"

"Yeah. She has a website. Just search for Janice Healy."

"Okay. I will," Paola said.

"How are your parents?"

"They're doing fine. My father's still working a few days a week, and my mother's still running the house. How are your parents?"

"They have health problems. My mother has a bad knee, and my father has a tricky heart, which suddenly goes into high gear for no apparent reason. He's now on medication, which seems to be helping. But my mother will probably have to get a knee replacement."

"Is she covered for that?"

"Oh, yeah. They have Medicare and a good supplement."

"My parents are covered by the healthcare plan of our business, and so am I, but it's getting more expensive."

"So is our plan. The premiums keep going up."

"Well, let's have lunch during your Christmas break. We could go to D & V."

"That sounds good. And let me know how it goes with Janice."

"I will. And thanks."

After ending the call she went into her bedroom where she kept her computer. In the house there had been a room for an office, but she didn't have that luxury now. She went online and found the website of Janice Healy. It showed a woman in her sixties, who looked wise. It gave her credentials in psychology, which included a Ph.D. from Fordham. It didn't say she had been a nun. Her office was in Hastings, not far away.

She sat there for a while wondering when would be a good time to broach the idea with her daughter, who wouldn't get up the next morning until she had safely missed the twelve o'clock mass. By the time they returned from church, she might be gone. So now was probably a good time to go and talk with her.

Paola gently rapped on the door, and when there was no response she opened it and saw her daughter lying on her bed with her laptop, watching some kind of violent action on a video. She didn't understand the attraction of violence, especially since Briana was nonviolent in her behavior. Was this an outlet that she needed for her primal instincts? Did it make her feel close to her father who liked to watch the same kind of thing?

"Am I interrupting something important?"

"No, not really," Briana muttered.

"Can we talk?"

"Okay." Briana paused the video and rolled over, facing the wall as if it had precedence for her attention.

Looking for a way to begin, Paola said: "Do you remember Tina's mother?"

"Yeah. She's your best friend."

"She works with kids who have problems. At times they need help beyond what she can give them, so she knows a lot of therapists—"

"I know where you're going," Briana interrupted. "I don't want to see a therapist."

"She might be able to help you."

"I don't need help. I don't have a problem."

"We all have problems."

"Then why don't *you* see a therapist?"

"Do you want me to see one?"

"Yeah, I do. And maybe you'll get off my back."

She thought for a moment, and then she said: "If I see a therapist, will you see one?"

Briana shrugged noncommittally.

"I'll tell you what. I'll see the therapist that Tina's mother recommended for you, and then you can see her. Okay?"

There was a long silence toward the end of which Briana's shoulders started shaking, and finally she rolled over, facing Paola with tears streaming down her cheeks. And spitting the words, Briana said: "I hate you for what you did to Dad. I hate you!"

TWO

IT STARTED THE night when she and Gabby went to a bar on Lake Avenue to celebrate the fact that now they could both drink legally. Paola had turned twenty-one in April, and Gabby's birthday had been two days ago, and it was Friday, a night for working people to give thanks for the respite of the weekend.

Though there were a few dives in the area, O'Malley's was the only bar between Roberts Avenue and Lake Avenue where young people and families were comfortable. Of course it was Irish because the neighborhood was mainly Irish, and for Paola and Gabby going to a bar was a venture into another world. Their parents didn't go to bars and rarely even went to restaurants, believing you could always eat better at home.

At the time of their celebration Paola had just completed four years of apprenticeship at her father's business and Gabby had just completed her bachelor's degree at St. Catherine, so they had more than one occasion to recognize. But when they arrived at the door of O'Malley's and heard the din, they didn't quite have the courage to enter.

Then, from behind them, a guy walked around them and politely held the door open for them, saying: "Come in, ladies. You're welcome here."

So they went in and luckily found two seats at the end of the bar, where it made a corner.

Though there were a lot of people demanding his attention, the bartender came right over to them and said: "Hi, ladies. What'll ya have?"

"I'll have a Bud," Gabby said as if that was what she always had.

"You want a glass?"

"No, a bottle."

"I'll have the same," Paola said. She noticed that there were no other girls sitting at the bar, and the guys were all drinking beer out of bottles, so they had done the right thing.

There were booths along the wall opposite the bar, and there were tables in the middle where people were eating as well as drinking. Some girls were sitting in the booths and at the tables, but they were greatly outnumbered by guys. From their position at the end of the bar Paola and Gabby could take in the whole scene, and under the noise of people talking and music playing they had privacy to share their impressions while sipping beer.

"You see that blond girl in the booth?" Gabby said. "She goes to our church."

"She looks different here," Paola said.

"Yeah, she does. And the guy with her went to Sacred Heart."

"Oh, yeah. What's his name?"

"Johnny or Bobby or something like that."

"It's only four years ago, and we can't remember the guy's name."

"Well, we didn't hang out with him."

"No, we didn't." There was something about him that hadn't appealed to them. And here he was, with a pretty girl who went to their church.

After spotting a few other guys they recognized but didn't know, they noticed a round table in back with only guys sitting at it. They looked as if they owned the place. And they weren't drinking beer, they were drinking cocktails out of special glasses.

They didn't recognize any of these guys.

"They're older," Gabby said.

"How much older?"

"Four or five years. I mean, that guy who's losing his hair could be as old as thirty."

"Thirty? Oh, my god."

They both laughed.

Paola was losing interest in that table when a new arrival caught her attention. He was tall and lean, with dark curly hair. He was greeted by the guys at the table with a boisterous cheer as if he was the life of the party. He acknowledged them with a wave of his hand and then worked his way around the table to an empty chair, which they must have been saving for him.

When he turned around and she saw his face it was as if she had touched a live wire.

"What is it?" Gabby asked her.

"I don't know," she managed to reply after regaining speech.

Following her gaze, Gabby said: "It's that guy, right?"

She nodded. "Yeah."

"He's hot."

"Yeah."

"I don't recognize him. Do you?"

"No. I never saw him before." She finally cooled herself a little by taking a long sip of beer. "How old do you think he is?"

"A few years older. Maybe twenty-five."

She stopped gazing at him, afraid that he might notice her. She took another sip of beer and started another line of conversation. But her eyes kept going back to him.

"You want to meet him?" Gabby asked her.

"God, no. I wouldn't know what to say to him."

"Just tell him you're an electrician. That would throw him."

"It would? Why?"

"You don't look like an electrician."

"What do I look like?"

"The girl of his dreams."

"Oh, I don't think so. He looks Irish, and I'm not Irish."

"He doesn't dream about Irish girls. He sees enough of them in real life. He dreams about girls who are different."

"Am I different?"

"Yeah, you are. I bet he doesn't know any girls who are electricians."

For a while they both watched him from a safe distance. He was telling stories, entertaining the other guys, making them laugh. He was indeed the life of the party, and he was giving them a good time.

Though she didn't have room for it, Paola went along with another round of beer, and though they talked about other things, they kept returning to the subject of the guy, who was still entertaining the other guys. They speculated on what he did for a living. With his tanned face, he didn't look like someone who worked in an office. And he probably didn't drive a truck. He probably worked in the open air.

"Maybe he's a cop," Paola said.

"Naw, he doesn't look like a cop," Gabby said. "He looks like he does something physical."

"Then maybe he works in construction."

"Yeah. Maybe he does."

They stayed another hour, dragging out the second round of beer. They watched to see if anything would happen that would tell them more about the guy, but he kept regaling the other guys with stories, making them laugh.

"You know," Gabby said, "he could be a stand-up comedian."

"Oh, I hope not," Paola said.

"What's wrong with that?"

"It's not a stable occupation."

"Hey, you're getting ahead of things."

"I'm only speculating."

Gabby looked at the guy and then looked at Paola. "Yeah, I guess I can see the two of you together."

"I can't see that," Paola said. "I can only imagine it."

They agreed to return to O'Malley's the following Friday, but it was a long week for Paola. She was working with Benny, a guy who had been with her father for twenty-five years and knew everything about the business. He was too old for contracting work, so he was assigned to the calls they got from homeowners who needed repairs or new installations, and since she wasn't yet allowed to work on her own, she accompanied Benny and learned from him.

Their range included all of Yonkers plus the river villages from Hastings to Tarrytown, so they spent a lot of time driving from one job to another. Each day an office manager, whose name was Clara, devised a route for them that would minimize the distance they traveled, but it never quite worked out that way because they didn't know how long it would take to do a job or whether the person who was supposed to be at home would actually be there. Some of the jobs were straightforward, like rewiring a box with an overloaded circuit breaker, but some of them were complex, like the one on Wednesday at a house in Hastings where the problem was an overhead light in a closet on the second floor. The owner, a man in his seventies, who knew a little about electricity, had changed the bulb, but that hadn't solved the problem. The first thing that Benny did, with Paola watching, was check the switch, but that worked fine. So the problem was somewhere in the wiring, which would be difficult to find because the wire to the light ran above the ceiling and the wire to the switch ran inside the wall, and the house was more than a hundred years old, so the ceiling and the wall were lath and plaster.

Benny asked the man if he knew where the wire to the switch came from. The man wasn't sure, but he thought it came from the third floor, which wasn't finished and still had the original rough boards that could be easily pried up for gaining access to spaces under the floor and inside the walls, through which they had run wires.

"Are there boxes under that floor?" Benny asked.

"Yeah, there are several," the man said. He looked upward from the switch and pointed to the ceiling. "The box for this wire is probably right above us."

"Let's go up and see."

The three of them climbed the steep stairs to the third floor, which the man used as an office. The middle of the floor was covered by a worn Persian rug, and around its edges were rough boards that looked as if they had never been painted.

The man knelt and touched a board, saying: "It should be under here."

"Can I pry it up?" Benny asked him.

"Yeah, sure. You can see that it's been pried up before."

In fact, the board had been cut to a three-foot length, and with his screwdriver Benny easily pried it up. In the space below, between the beams, there was a box.

"That should be it," Benny said. He knelt and started turning a screw in the box's cover.

Paola watched as he uncovered the box and found the junction between two wires.

"Can you turn off the power for this box?"

"Yeah. It's in the basement. I don't know which circuit breaker it is, so I'll have to try them. Let me know when the power's off."

"Paola, go down to the second floor and relay our messages."

That was her first contribution to this job, but while she was waiting for Benny to yell down that the power was off, her mind strayed. She thought about the guy at O'Malley's, and she hoped he would be there on Friday.

After relaying their messages she returned to the third floor and watched Benny unwrap the tape from the connection. "The wires came loose, you see?"

She bent down and saw that the two wires were not connected. "How did that happen?"

"It must have been vibrations from people walking on these boards. But if the job had been done properly, they wouldn't have come loose."

Along with the man, who had returned out of breath, she watched Benny do the job properly. He sent the man back down to the basement to turn on the power, while Paola went down to the second floor to try the light, her second contribution.

"The power's on," the man yelled.

She tried the light and yelled up to Benny: "The light works."

On Friday she and Gabby took the same seats at the end of the bar and ordered beers and began talking about what had happened to them during the week. Gabby was working five days a week as a counselor at a camp for inner-city children at St. Catherine. She loved the work, which was related to her future career, and though the job didn't pay very well, she was able to save money for graduate school, which she was going to start that fall. She was leery of incurring debt to pay the tuition, but there was no other way, other than a graduate assistantship that would pay for some of it. Paola, with her father's encouragement, had begun to think about going to college and getting a degree in business administration, which he believed would help her when she took over from him. But that day was far in the future, so she had put it off for another year.

They were deep in conversation when the door opened and the guy walked in. For some reason he turned in their direction, and his happy blue eyes engaged with hers. Reflexively, she smiled at him, and he smiled back at her, raising her hopes. But he kept going and joined his buddies at the round table.

"I saw the way he smiled at you," Gabby told her.

"Oh, I don't think it meant anything. He didn't stop to talk with us."

"I think he'd rather hang out with guys."

"You think he's gay?"

"No, I just think he has such a good time hanging out with guys, he doesn't want to bother with girls."

She thought about it. "My brothers usually hang out with guys. Occasionally they go out with girls, but they don't have relationships with girls."

"I think most guys are that way."

"Well, I don't care if they'd rather hang out with each other. What do we need them for?"

"Making babies," Gabby said. "But that's about all. And I'm not planning to make a baby any time soon."

She put the guy out of her mind, and they resumed talking about other things. A while later they were talking about their parents when she sensed that a person was approaching from behind her. Without looking, she knew who it was, and when she turned, there he was, only a few feet away from her.

"Hey, ladies," he said, with bright blue eyes. "How are you doing?"

"We're doing fine," Gabby told him.

"I haven't seen you here before. Where are you from?"

"We're from the Bronx."

"You're kidding," he said, with his eyes even brighter. "What part of the Bronx?"

"I *was* kidding," Gabby admitted. "We're not from the Bronx. We're from around here."

"Well, I'm from the Bronx. That's why I was interested. Where are you from around here?"

"Over near St. Brigid."

"I know that church. I went there for a wedding. That's not around here."

"It's only a half mile away."

"You walk here?"

"No. We have a car."

"You mean the car belongs to both of you?"

"No. It belongs to me. But we both came here in my car."

Looking straight at Paola, he asked: "Do you talk?"

"Yeah, I talk," she managed to say.

"Then say something."

"I'm an electrician."

That did throw him. For a moment he was speechless, and then he said; "You're kidding."

"I'm not kidding."

"She's not kidding," Gabby confirmed.

"You work with hot wires?"

"We usually turn off the power before we work with them."

He gazed at her in admiration. "You know what? I work with hot wires too."

"Are you an electrician?"

"I'm a lineman for the electric company."

So they had been right about him working outdoors, and she imagined him climbing a pole as she had seen guys doing in her neighborhood. "You work around here?"

"I work wherever they send me, but mainly in Yonkers. That's why I live in Yonkers."

"Where in Yonkers?"

"Just down the street, above the pharmacy."

"That must be handy," Gabby said.

"Yeah, we can get into the store any time and help ourselves."

"Then if we need anything, you can get it for us."

"No problem," the guy said with a straight face. He motioned to the bartender, who came right over. "Could you give them another round on me?"

"Yeah, boss," the bartender said.

"Have you lived here long?" Gabby asked him.

"I've lived here almost five years. And I know everyone except you guys. How come you were never here before?"

"We just became legal."

He cocked his head. "You waited until you were legal?"

"Yeah. We didn't want to get into trouble."

"You must be Catholic school girls."

"We went to Sacred Heart. But what does that have to do with it?"

"You were conditioned to obey rules."

"The drinking age isn't a rule, it's a law."

He nodded. "Yeah. That's a good distinction. So you don't mind breaking rules."

"It depends on the rule," Gabby said. "It also depends on the situation."

At that moment the bartender placed two more bottles of Bud on the counter, and Paola took one and sipped the cold beer. She was glad that her friend was engaging him, which gave her a chance to observe him without being the center of his attention. But she felt that while he was talking to Gabby he was putting on a show for her.

"Thanks for the drink," Gabby said.

"Yeah, thanks," Paola said.

"It's my pleasure. What are you names?"

"I'm Gabriella."

"I'm Paola."

"You're not Irish, but you went to Sacred Heart, so you must be Italian."

"We're actually Russian, so watch out."

"Well, I'm Chinese, so I have you outnumbered."

"What's your name?" Gabby asked.

"It's Daniel, but everyone calls me Danny."

"Like Danny boy in that sad Irish song?"

"You want to hear me sing it?"

"No," Gabby told him, covering her ears with her hands.

Ignoring her, Danny rose to his tiptoes and crooned the first line: "Oh, Danny boy, the pipes, the pipes are call-all-ing."

He had a lovely tenor voice, and Paola hoped he would keep singing, but he abruptly stopped as if he had only wanted to give them a sample of his talent.

Gabby got up from her barstool, saying: "Excuse me. I gotta go to the ladies' room."

"I hope it wasn't my singing," Danny said.

"No, I don't have to throw up. I only have to pee."

Paola thought of going with her friend, but she was afraid that while they were gone Danny would return to the guys at the table in back, so she remained on her barstool. But alone with him, she didn't know what to talk about.

He helped by asking: "Where do you work as an electrician?"

"I work for my father at Borgatti Electric."

"Oh, yeah," he said. "I've seen your trucks. So next time I see a Borgatti truck, you might be riding in it?"

"I might be driving it. I work with a guy who thinks he's too old to drive."

"Then I don't have to worry about him?"

She thought she understood what he meant, and it rattled her, but she recovered enough to say: "I'm not dating him."

"Are you dating anyone?"

"Not right now."

"Then how about you and Gabriella joining me and my roommate tomorrow night?"

"You can call her Gabby. Who's your roommate?"

"That guy on the left side of the table," he said, pointing to a guy with light brown hair. "His name is Ron."

"How do you know he'll like Gabby?"

"He likes girls who kid around."

"Well, when she comes back we can ask her."

As soon as Gabby rejoined them, Danny repeated his invitation and pointed again to Ron, who at that moment was laughing at something.

Gabby coolly appraised him, saying: "I've seen worse looking guys."

"What do you mean? There are people who think he looks like Robert Redford."

"Maybe he does, but that doesn't do anything for me."

"So are you with us or not?"

Gabby found Paola's hand and took it. "Yeah, I'm with you."

Paola understood that her friend was only doing this for her, and she squeezed her hand to thank her.

Since it wasn't a formal date, they met at O'Malley's, where the guys arrived ahead of them and occupied the end of the bar. The plan was to have a drink at O'Malley's and then drive over to Brennan's and have dinner. Brennan's was an Irish pub on McLean Avenue, and it had been the home base for Danny and Ron before they moved to Lake Avenue.

They went in Danny's car, which was parked on the street near O'Malley's, facing west toward Palisade Avenue. Just before Paola reached the door, Danny moved there ahead of her, and with a flourish he opened it for her.

"Thanks," she said, trying to remember the last time anyone had opened a door for her.

Ron did likewise for Gabby, who said: "You guys are such gentlemen."

"We were well raised," Danny said.

"By nuns," Ron added. "If we didn't behave, they beat the shit out of us."

"Oh, that's a myth," Gabby said. "I never saw a nun hit a kid."

"You didn't go to school in the Bronx."

"And that's another myth. You think the Bronx was the only tough place to grow up?"

By now the car was in motion, and after going a short distance Danny did a U-turn and headed east to Vineyard Avenue, where he turned right. Paola knew the way because for her job she had often driven around in this area.

While Gabby and Ron sparred in the back seat, Paola asked Danny: "Where in the Bronx did you grow up?"

"Woodlawn," he said.

She had done a few jobs in Woodlawn, so she knew where it was. It was an Irish neighborhood, and based on her experience with a homeowner who had such a thick brogue she had trouble understanding him, there were people in Woodlawn who had recently immigrated from Ireland.

"Did your parents come from Ireland?"

"My Dad did. He came here when he was fifteen."

"What did he do for a living?"

"He worked as a lineman for the company. I followed in his footsteps." The way he said this, she could tell he felt blessed to have followed in his father's footsteps, and she didn't have to ask if he liked his job. She could tell he loved it.

"How old were you when you started working there?"

"I was eighteen, just like my father."

"How long have you been working there?"

"Are you trying to figure out how old I am?"

"I don't care how old you are as long as you're not over thirty."

"I'm not over thirty. Do I look that old?"

"No, but you act like you have a lot of experience."

"I guess I do. I've been supporting myself for seven years."

So Gabby had guessed it: he was twenty-five. "You said you've lived on Lake Avenue for almost five years."

"Yeah, that's right."

"Then you must have left your parents' home when you were twenty."

"You're good at math," he said, turning left onto Myrtle Street.

"Actually, I'm not good at math. I almost flunked it in high school. But at least I can add and subtract."

"In case you're wondering," he said after a silence, "I didn't leave my parents' home because I didn't get along with them. I love my parents. But I was ready to be on my own, and I felt that my parents deserved a rest after raising five children."

"Were you the youngest?"

"Yeah, I was the baby. They kept trying to have a boy, and they kept having girls, so when I arrived it was like they hit the jackpot."

"Did your sisters spoil you?"

"Yeah, I was a live doll for them. But I survived."

"I'm the youngest in our family. I have two older brothers. And I survived."

After turning right on Nepperhan Avenue he asked: "Do your older brothers work for the family business?"

"No. They didn't want to have anything to do with it."

"Then you had no choice?"

"I had a choice. And I chose to be an electrician. I didn't want to be a teacher or a nurse or a secretary or a flight attendant."

"One of my sisters is a secretary, and she hates it."

"She does? What do your other sisters do?"

"Two are married and have children and stay at home, at least for now. The other joined the navy, and she loves it."

"I might have done that if I hadn't decided to be an electrician."

"Yeah, you could have been an electrician in the navy."

"That's where our family business is," she said, pointing to the building. "We have a parking lot in back for the trucks."

"I did a job in this area. A guy who was drunk out of his mind ran his car into a pole and knocked it over. The whole area lost power."

"What happened to him?"

"He wasn't hurt. He drove away, and it took the police a few days to catch him."

They turned left onto Yonkers Avenue and followed it to Midland Avenue, which they took as far south as McLean Avenue, where they headed east.

"Where are we?" Gabby asked from the back seat.

"We're still in Yonkers," Ron said.

"We are? It feels like the Bronx."

"We don't have far to go," Danny assured her. "And yeah, we're getting close to the Bronx."

On her job Paola had driven past Brennan's, but at night it was all lit up, and it looked different. It looked like a lot was happening there.

Danny somehow found a parking spot, and he led them into the place. He was greeted by the guys at the bar with a raucous cheer as if he was a hero returning from a faraway land. And he reciprocated by high-fiving several of them.

"We have a reservation," he told the hostess, a pretty blond.

"What's the name?" she asked, pretending she didn't know who he was.

"Danny O'Dwyer. There're four of us."

She led them to an empty table in a prime location, where they sat down.

Within a minute a waiter brought them menus. With a thick brogue like the man that Paola had done the job for, he said: "It's good to see you lads. It's been a while."

"Yeah, almost a month," Danny said. "How are you doing?"

"I'm doing fine. What'll you have to drink, ladies?"

"I'll have a glass of white wine," Gabby said.

"I'll have one too," Paola said, having no idea how it would taste. On special occasions her father drank a glass or two of red wine, but never white wine.

The waiter didn't ask the guys, evidently knowing what they drank, and he left them, giving them time to peruse the menus.

"They have good food here," Danny said.

There were items on the menu that were unfamiliar to Paola, and curious, she asked: "What's shepherd's pie?"

"It's hamburger meat and mashed potatoes. I don't think you'd like it. But I think you'd like the fish and chips."

"What's that?"

"It's fried fish and French fries."

"What are you having?"

"I feel like a steak. You can have a steak if you want."

"No. I couldn't eat a whole steak."

"I'll have the fish and chips," Gabby said, closing her menu.

"I'll have that too," Paola said. Though at the last minute she noticed that they also had pasta, she believed it wouldn't be as good as her mother's.

Afterward she couldn't remember much of what they talked about, but they got along well, and they had a good time. Ron and Gabby traded good-natured barbs, and Danny told stories that made them laugh. In fact, though she considered herself a happy girl, she had never laughed so much in her life, and she could understand why Danny was popular. He made the people around him happy, he made them forget the things in their lives that caused them stress, he made the sun come out for them.

Around midnight he drove them home, first Gabby and then her. Ron accompanied Gabby to the door of her house, and Paola averted her eyes from seeing whether they kissed each other goodnight. When Danny stopped with her at the door he hesitated, and somehow she let him know it was all right to kiss her, which he did very tenderly. And just like when she first saw his face, it was as if she had touched a live wire.

THREE

DURING THAT SUMMER the four of them went out together every Saturday. They mostly went to Brennan's, but they also did other things, which included a Yankees game on a perfect night at the stadium. And they went to Jones Beach, where the guys took them to a stretch of sand that wasn't so crowded. There at the beach Paola saw Danny's body for the first time, and she was amazed by how lithe it was. Ron was more solid, but they both had great bodies, which of course they showed off by passing a Frisbee back and forth at the edge of the sand. At one point Danny led her by the hand into the ocean and through the surf to where they could float in the rising and falling water, with their limbs gently grazing each other. And afterwards they lay on a big towel that he had brought, together side by side in the benign sun.

When he drove her home at the end of the evening he always walked her to the door and kissed her goodnight. It was the same kind of kiss as he had given her the first time, tender and warm and promising, and it had the same effect on her. She kept hoping that it would last longer and go deeper, but he always managed to stop short of her expectations. And he always left her wanting more.

On Fridays the two girls continued going to O'Malley's to celebrate the end of the work week, and one night near the end of the summer Gabby said: "I'm going out with Ron tomorrow, but after that I'm done with him."

"You're tired of him?"

"I'm not tired of him, but he wants me to be his girlfriend, and I don't feel that way about him. I explained that to him, but he still thinks I might change how I feel. And I know I won't change, so I don't want to lead him on."

"I understand."

"Besides, I'm going to start graduate school next week, and I won't have as much time for socializing."

"I hope you'll have time for us."

"Oh, yeah. I'll always have time for us. But I don't need a guy in my life."

She sipped her beer considering the prospect of going out alone with Danny. After always being in a foursome with him it would be different being alone with him, and she had mixed feelings about that situation. She could see how it might allow their relationship to develop at another level, but having always seen him in a context of other people, she was afraid that being alone with her wouldn't be enough for him.

They met at O'Malley's on their first date without another couple. Since she didn't have a car, Paola walked over to Palisade Avenue, where she could catch a bus to Lake Avenue. She had to wait almost ten minutes for the bus, and the bus trip took about fifteen minutes, so it was about a half hour from her house to O'Malley's. But that wasn't bad, and riding on the bus she had a chance to prepare herself for an evening alone with Danny.

When she arrived at O'Malley's he was standing at the end of the bar, waiting for her, and he led her to the round table in back, where two seats had evidently been saved for them. He introduced her to the guys around the table, proudly informing them that she was an electrician, and he got her to talk with them about her work. He made her feel like a member of his group, and she appreciated his consideration. But at the same time she wondered if he wanted to avoid being alone with her.

When he drove her home he didn't get out of the car but sat there for a while before he asked: "Why did Gabby break up with Ron?"

"She didn't break up with him. They were just friends."

"Does she like him?"

"Yeah. She likes him fine."

"Then why doesn't she want to go out with him?"

"He wants to be more than friends, and she doesn't want to."

After a silence he asked: "Are we more than friends?"

"You mean you don't know?" she said, surprised by his question.

"Well, *I* feel like we're more than friends, but I don't know how *you* feel."

"You can't tell from the way I kiss you?"

"I guess I can, but I don't know."

Without another word, she leaned toward him and gave him a kiss to settle the question.

When she finally pulled away he gazed at her, speechless, and not wanting to break the spell, she opened the door and got out and strode to her house. Before letting herself in she turned and saw him in the same position where she had left him, immobile at the wheel of his car.

Lying in bed that night, she thought about what had happened. She understood that she had wanted to prove something to him, and it looked as if she had succeeded. But if she hadn't, would she have to go farther? Did she want to go farther?

With two older brothers, she had always believed she knew a lot about guys, but now she was in an area where she didn't have much experience. She had gone out on dates, but with those guys there was no electricity. She had kissed a few of them, only to see what it was like, and it hadn't turned her on. And unlike girls, they weren't fun to talk with, even though she shared their interest in sports.

Still, she thought a lot about sex. It was hard not to, with provocative images and messages coming at her from all directions. And she had fantasies, which usually involved a hot singer or a hot actor. But they had nothing to do with reality. They were safely removed from any of the guys she encountered in her daily life.

This guy was different. He wasn't a guy from her daily life, and he wasn't a phantom from her imagination. He was a real guy, whom she had met in an Irish pub, and with him there was electricity. The sight of his face and the touch of his lips set off a powerful reaction within her. There wasn't much about her feelings that she didn't understand, but there was a lot about *his* feelings that she didn't understand. Since he was such a hot guy, he should have had a lot of experience with girls, and yet tonight he acted as if he didn't know very much about them. He acted as if he wasn't comfortable being alone with her. Then in the car he revealed that he wasn't sure about her feelings. He also revealed that he cared about her feelings. And most important, he revealed his own feelings. At least he had said he felt like they were more than friends.

Rolling over, she wondered if he was serious about her, or if she was only the latest in a series of girls who fell for him and gave him whatever he wanted until he got tired of them and moved on to the next one. To settle this question, she needed to learn his history, not only from him but also from one of those girls.

For the next several weeks they met on Saturday at O'Malley's, where they spent the evening in a group. The group was usually only guys, with occasionally a girl other than Paola. Among them were guys who worked at the electric company and the phone company, and guys who were carpenters, plumbers, or mechanics. None of them was married, but some of them had girlfriends, whom they evidently saw later in the evening. They stayed for a few drinks, and then they left, replaced by other guys who joined the group. Paola and Danny usually left around midnight, and by then the place was filling with workers from other restaurants that closed earlier than O'Malley's.

When he drove her home they always lingered for a while in the car, extending the realm of kissing and fondling, up to a limit. According to what her mother had told her, she was the one who was supposed to set the limit, but he was the one who actually set the limit, stopping before she made him stop, which always left her wanting more.

One evening, in the middle of October, they were sitting in a group at the round table when Ron came over from the bar, where he had been standing with a girl. From their body language Paola could tell that the girl and Ron had something going, and from what she overheard when Ron leaned over and asked Danny something, Ron wanted to take the girl to their apartment. She didn't hear their full conversation, but she gathered that it was okay with Danny.

They stayed at O'Malley's for at least an hour after Ron and the girl left, and then Danny paid the tab. As he was getting change from the bartender, Paola noticed a long-haired girl sitting at the end of the bar where she and Gabby usually sat. The girl, seeing that Paola was with Danny, gave her a look of sympathy.

As usual they lingered in the car before Danny walked her to the door, and after kissing him goodnight she entered the house, where she found her grandmother standing in the hallway, waiting up for her.

"Nonna," she said. "Are you all right?"

"Yes, *I'm* all right," her grandmother said, inspecting her. "But I'm worried about *you*."

"What are you worried about?"

"I saw what you were doing in that boy's car."

"We were just kissing."

"Well, you were in his car for a long time," her grandmother said. "If you were just kissing each other goodnight, you could have done that at the door."

"Don't worry. We weren't doing anything wrong." She kissed her grandmother on the cheek. "You should go to bed now. It's after midnight."

"I know what time it is," her grandmother said as if she wasn't just talking about the time. "Be careful."

"I will be."

As she went upstairs she remembered the look of sympathy from that girl at the bar which, together with her grandmother's warning, made her uneasy. And she wondered what they knew about life that she didn't know.

The next evening, as she was helping her mother clean up after dinner, drying the dishes and putting them away in the cabinet, her mother said: "I hear you have a boyfriend."

"Did you hear that from Nonna?"

"Yeah, I did. She saw you with a boy in his car."

"She saw us kissing. Does she think I'll get pregnant from kissing?"

"She knows what kissing can lead to."

"Well, don't worry. It's not going to lead to anything," she said, taking a wet plate. "I'm never alone with him."

"You were alone with him in his car, weren't you?"

"Yeah, but we were parked in front of our house. If we were going to do anything, we'd park somewhere else."

"I guess you would." Her mother washed another plate. "If you're never alone with him, what do you do?"

"We hang out at O'Malley's."

"Is that the bar on Lake Avenue?"

"It's also a restaurant."

"What's his name?"

"Danny."

"Is he Irish?"

"Yeah. How did you guess?"

"He hangs out at bars, and that's what the Irish like to do."

"Well, maybe that was true when you were young, but everyone hangs out at bars now."

Her mother reached for the dish soap and squeezed a few drops onto her sponge. "I hope you don't drink a lot."

"I don't. I only have a few beers."

"Does he drink a lot?"

"No, he actually doesn't. He's too busy entertaining his friends."

"Does he have a lot of friends?"

"Yeah. He knows everyone."

"And how does he entertain his friends?"

"He tells them stories, and he makes them laugh."

"How old is he?"

"He's twenty-five."

"Does he have a job?"

"Of course. He's a lineman for the electric company."

"You mean he climbs poles?"

"They don't climb poles anymore. They use cherry pickers."

"Cherry pickers?"

"I don't know why they're called cherry pickers. Maybe they're for picking cherries. But they're also called bucket trucks."

"Oh, yeah. The machines that lift the men in buckets to work on the poles."

"That's right. You've seen them."

"Does his job pay well?"

"I think it does. He's never short of money."

"Where does he live?"

"In Yonkers. He has an apartment on Lake Avenue."

"Does he live by himself?"

"No, he has a roommate."

"I'm glad he has a roommate," her mother said, rinsing a dish and handing it to her.

Paola understood: the roommate was an obstacle that would prevent her from being alone with the guy in his apartment.

"Is he from Yonkers?"

"No, he's from the Bronx."

"What part of the Bronx?"

"Woodlawn."

"That's an Irish neighborhood."

"Yeah, I know."

"Does he have brothers and sisters?"

"He has four sisters."

"Four sisters?" Her mother obviously felt that this was a good thing. "Is he the oldest?"

"No, he's the youngest."

"Then he must have been spoiled by his sisters."

"Well, he doesn't act like he was spoiled. In fact, he's very considerate of people."

Her mother handed the last wet dish to her.

"So now you know as much as I know about him," Paola said, drying the dish. "It's not a serious relationship, and I don't expect it to last long."

"That's good," her mother said. "You're too young to have a serious relationship."

When they were done she left the kitchen and went to her room, wondering if she really *was* too young to have a serious relationship. Maybe Danny felt she was too young, and that was his reason for holding back. Or maybe he felt they were both too young.

She lay on her bed and thought about her parents. Her father was thirty when he got married, and her mother was almost twenty-five. So she could understand why her mother felt she was too young. And now people were marrying later than her parents' generation, which added weight to the argument that she was too young. But what if you were too young when you met the right guy? Were you supposed to forego the opportunity?

She laughed at herself for being so silly. As revealed in her conversation with her mother, she didn't know enough about Danny to determine if he was the right guy. She was strongly attracted to him, but she didn't have a serious relationship with him. Before you could have a serious relationship with a guy, you had to get to know him. And the only way you could get to know him was to spend time alone with him.

On Friday she and Gabby were at O'Malley's, sitting at their usual places, when the long-haired girl approached and sat down next to her, saying: "Hi. I'm Sondra."

"I'm Paola," she said, to be friendly. "And this is Gabby."

"I've seen you here before."

"Yeah, we're here every Friday."

"You were here last Saturday. It looked like you were with Danny O'Dwyer."

"I *was* with him," Paola said, afraid that this girl was somehow going to claim him.

"How long have you been seeing him?"

"I don't know. About four months."

"Wow, that's a record." Sondra said, making a gesture of applause.

"What do you mean?"

"I've known Danny for a long time, and I don't remember any of his girls lasting more than six weeks."

"Were you one of them?"

"Oh, yeah. I lasted six weeks. I had the record." Sondra didn't sound unhappy that another girl had broken her record. She only sounded amazed by it.

Gabby, who had been listening, entered the conversation and asked: "Are you saying that he's a serial lover?"

"Danny? A serial lover?" Sondra laughed as if the idea was preposterous. "Oh, not at all. I'm only saying he doesn't last long with girls."

"I thought you said it was the girls who didn't last long," Paola pointed out.

"They don't, but he doesn't last long either."

"Do the girls break up with him," Gabby asked, "or does he break up with them?"

"That's a good question," Sondra said. "In my case, I broke up with him."

"Why did you break up with him?"

"I got tired of waiting to be alone with him."

"You were always in a group with him?"

"Yeah, always. And I began to feel I was only a member of his group."

"Did you have sex with him?"

Smiling thinly, Sondra said: "You get right to the point."

"Yeah, I do," Gabby said, smiling thinly back.

"The truth is, I didn't have sex with him."

"Did you want to have sex with him?"

"Of course I did. He's a hot guy."

"Then why didn't you have sex with him?"

"I was never alone with him."

"You couldn't ever get him away from the group?"

"No, I couldn't. And I didn't want to have sex with him on the table with all those guys sitting around it."

"That's because you were well raised."

They all laughed.

"If he only wants to be with guys," Paola asked, "then why does he take out girls?"

"I have no idea," Sondra said. "For some reason, he needs them. But I'm not a psychologist, so I can't tell you why."

"What *are* you?" Gabby asked. "What do you do?"

"I'm a graphic artist. I work for a marketing firm in the city."

"I'm studying to be a psychologist, but I don't know why he takes out girls. I think he needs them as members of his group."

"Yeah, that's how I feel," Paola said, "like a member of his group. And I wonder if he knows what else to do with me."

"He has four older sisters," Sondra said. "He should know about girls."

"Maybe he knows too much about them," Gabby said.

"Well, based on my experience, I think he wants to avoid getting entangled with them."

"That's true of most guys."

"Yeah, it is. But most guys don't go to such lengths to avoid being alone with girls. In fact, they *want* to be alone with girls so they can have sex with them."

"But if they have sex with them, they get entangled with them."

"They do, but when their balls take over they don't worry about getting entangled."

Gabby nodded. "They don't worry about anything."

For a while they were silent, feeling as if they had gotten to the bottom of things, and then with her hand on Paola's shoulder, Sondra said: "You've lasted four months with him, girl. So maybe it'll be different with you."

The next day, which was Saturday, she met him at O'Malley's. As usual, she got there first, and she was sitting at the end of the bar, sipping beer, when he arrived. Before he could take her to the round table, she said: "Let's do something different tonight."

"Like what?" he asked, looking perplexed.

"Oh, I don't know. We could have dinner at an Italian restaurant."

"I don't know any Italian restaurants."

"I do. In fact, there's a good one near my house."

He shrugged. "Okay. If that's what you want."

They left O'Malley's and walked to his car, which was parked on the street near his building.

He knew the way to her house, so she didn't have to give him directions, and he found a parking place near the restaurant.

D & V was owned by a family that her father knew, and it was one of the few places where her parents would eat out. It didn't have many tables, and on Saturday night of course it was packed, but the hostess, a daughter of the owner whom Paola had gone to school with, promised them a table within twenty minutes, so they sat at the bar that was used only by people waiting for tables, and they had a drink there. Paola had a glass of white wine and Danny had a bottle of Bud after ruling out Peroni.

"Do you eat here with your family?" Danny asked her after taking in the scene.

"Yeah. We eat here a few times a month. We've been coming here since I was a baby."

"Your parents brought you here as a baby?"

"Yeah. It's not a bar, it's a restaurant."

"So you sat at one of those tables as a family?"

"My mother likes that table there," she said, pointing to a table at the front window.

"We used to go to a restaurant in Woodlawn, my parents and my four sisters and me. We went there on Sunday after church."

"Do you still go there?"

"To the restaurant or church?"

"Either," she said.

"I meet them once or twice a month at the restaurant. After the noon mass," he added, "which I don't attend."

"Do your sisters still go to the restaurant?"

"The oldest and the youngest go there sometimes. The one who's a secretary lives in the city and has other things to do. And the one in the navy we don't see very often."

"The oldest and the youngest are the ones who are married, right?" she guessed.

"Right. They always bring their kids, which my parents are really crazy about."

She took a sip of wine. "So you don't go to church?"

"No, I don't. I probably would if I still lived with my family. I'd feel I had to go with them."

"I understand. I feel I have to go with my parents. But I also *need* to go to church."

"I think girls need it more than guys do."

"I think you're right. I wonder why."

"Well, maybe because girls have more complicated lives."

"You learned that from having four sisters?"

"Oh, yeah. There was always something with my sisters. We hardly ever had any peace and quiet in our house."

"Is that why you moved to Yonkers? To have peace and quiet?"

"It was one of the reasons."

"What were the other reasons?"

"I don't know. I wanted to be free and independent. I wanted to have my own life."

"Do you feel you've achieved your goal?"

"Are you interviewing me?" he asked with a smile.

"I'm sorry. But we're always in a group, so I haven't had a chance to ask these questions."

"And you really want to know the answers?"

"I really do."

They exchanged a look that was more intimate than anything they had done in his car.

"Okay," he finally said. "I feel I've achieved my goal. But now I'm beginning to wonder if there's more to life than hanging out at bars."

"There probably is," she said lightly, having found hope in his admission.

"But I don't know what it might be."

"It might be having dinner at an Italian restaurant. It looks like our table is ready."

Their table was against the side wall, as private as it could be in this room. At least it wasn't a round table with a group of guys.

"I don't know much about Italian food," he said, looking at his menu. "I know Italian wedges and spaghetti with meatballs, but that's about all."

"What would you like?"

"I'd like some meat."

"They have a good steak. I've never had it, but my brothers have, and they say it's good."

"Do your brothers still come here?"

She laughed. "Are *you* interviewing *me* now?"

"Well, we're always in a group," he mimicked her, "so I haven't had a chance to ask these questions."

"Yeah, they still come here. One of them lives in Hastings, and the other lives in Dobbs Ferry, so they're not far away."

"But they got out of Yonkers."

"They couldn't wait to get out of Yonkers."

"What about you?"

"I was born here, I grew up here, I live here, and I work here. I'm a Yonkers girl."

"Then you don't want to get out of Yonkers?"

"Why would I? Where would I go?"

"I don't know. I used to feel that way about the Bronx, but here I am in Yonkers. With a Yonkers girl," he added, smiling.

"You know what you want?" the waitress asked them.

Paola ordered the ravioli and with her encouragement Danny ordered the steak, medium, with a side order of pasta. She had another white wine, and he had another beer. She could only imagine him taking the step to red wine.

After dinner they returned to O'Malley's and hung out for a while at the round table, so her evening had a balance of being alone with Danny and being in a group with him.

Mindful of her grandmother's watchful eyes, she didn't linger in the car with him when he drove her home. She got out and let him walk her to the door, where he gave her a tender goodnight kiss.

"You know," he said as if he had made a discovery. "I liked

having dinner with you. And I liked the Italian food. We should do that again."

"Yeah, we should."

She walked up the stairs feeling they had moved forward in their relationship and beginning to have an idea of where they might go.

For the next several weeks and into December they went to dinner at an Italian restaurant, not only D & V but also one near St. John's Hospital and one in Dobbs Ferry. Alone with him, she got to know him as an individual instead of as a leader of a group. Behind his public front she found a thoughtful, sensitive guy. Instead of only being attracted to him, she was gradually falling in love with him, and the more she got to know him, the more she believed that Danny could be the right guy, and that she could make a commitment to him.

One night, in the middle of December, when they drove back to Lake Avenue after having dinner at D & V, instead of going to O'Malley's he suggested going to his apartment. He explained that Ron was planning to spend the night with his girlfriend at her apartment, so they would have the place to themselves.

By now she completely trusted Danny, so she had no problem with going to his apartment. In fact, she preferred the idea to being in a group at the round table. And she was curious about the place where Danny lived.

It was only three doors down the street from O'Malley's, on the second floor above the pharmacy. She followed Danny up the stairs and into a living room that was furnished with a sofa, two easy chairs, and a large-screen television. Against a far wall was a dining table with two simple chairs.

"We only sleep here," Danny said.

"You must also watch television," she said.

"We only watch sports, but the games are usually over by the time we get home, so we don't see much of them. Anyway, it's more fun to watch them at bars."

She wandered across the floor, which had no carpets. The

wood, which had seen better days, was painted brown. "Do you guys ever cook?"

"Well, we have a kitchen, but we only use it to make coffee and toast bagels."

She went into the kitchen, where she expected to see a mess. But there was nothing on the counter and nothing in the sink. "Who cleans up?"

"We both do. We share responsibilities."

Luckily, they didn't seem to have many responsibilities to share beyond rinsing out coffee mugs, which lay in the draining rack.

"Do you ever eat dinner here?"

"No, it's easier to eat out." He paused. "Oh, wait. Sometimes we do eat dinner here. We have takeout Chinese."

"You don't have pizza?"

"We sometimes do, but not very often."

She wandered back to the living room, where the obvious place to sit was the sofa.

"Would you like a glass of wine?"

"You have wine?"

"I got it for you. I thought we might come here eventually."

"Yeah, sure." She realized that he had done some planning for this situation, which didn't surprise her. It now seemed inevitable that they would come to his apartment.

"I'll bring it," he told her. "Make yourself at home."

She settled herself at one end of the sofa, which was more comfortable than it looked.

A grunt of effort came from the kitchen, where he must have been opening a bottle of wine. A few minutes later he emerged from the kitchen with a glass in one hand and a bottle in the other. He apologized, saying: "I don't have wine glasses."

"That's all right."

He handed her the glass, which was a juice glass, and he set the bottle on the floor.

She tasted the wine and nodded as if she knew what it was.

"Do you like it?"

"Yeah."

"I'll be right back."

While she sipped the wine he went to the kitchen and came back with a bottle of beer. For several minutes he paced in front of her, drinking the beer, but he finally sat down on the sofa, leaving space between them as if he didn't want her to think he was making a move.

"I'd play some music," he said after he was settled, "but our stereo stopped working, and we couldn't find anyone to fix it."

"Did you use it a lot?"

"No. We hardly ever used it."

"Then why did you buy it?"

"We didn't buy it. We got it from my oldest sister, who got a new one."

"We have a stereo. My brothers used it to play rock, and my parents couldn't stand it."

"My parents used ours to play Irish songs, and my sisters couldn't stand it. But that's how I learned 'Danny Boy'."

"From what I heard, you have a good voice."

"I didn't have any training, and I didn't even sing in the choir. But one of my uncles said I should have been a singer."

"It's a hard way to make a living."

"That's what my mother said. And I don't want to be a singer."

"What do you want to be?"

"I want to be a lineman."

"Can you imagine being anything else?"

"No, I can't. I *love* my job."

"Then you're lucky. From what I've heard, most people don't like their jobs."

"Do you like your job?"

"Yeah, I like it. I'm only an apprentice now, but when I finally get my license I think I'll like it even more."

"Will you love it?"

"Yeah, I think I will."

She had almost finished her second glass of wine when he leaned over and kissed her. At the touch of his lips she felt the usual charge of electricity, and released from the constraints of a car parked in front of her house and the vigilance of her grandmother, she let herself go.

By the time she realized that he wasn't going to stop himself, she was no longer in a position to stop him. And she didn't want to stop him.

<h1 style="text-align:center">FOUR</h1>

AFTER MAKING LOVE with him she felt that for her it was now a serious relationship, and she didn't have to wait long before she had reasons to believe it was serious for him. As he walked her to the door of her house that night he asked if he could see her on Wednesday. From the beginning they had only gone out on Saturdays, though on Fridays he always stopped and talked with her and Gabby at the bar, but now he wanted to see her more often, and since she wanted the same thing, she agreed to see him on Wednesday.

As usual she met him at O'Malley's, where there was a crowd of people taking a midweek break. They sat at the round table, they had burgers for dinner, and then they left. She wasn't surprised when he led her down the street toward his building. On the way, he explained that Ron was at his girlfriend's apartment for the night, so they would have the place to themselves, so at least he was letting her know in advance what he had in mind.

She settled herself on the sofa as she did the first time, but this time he had a wine glass for her, which he brought from the kitchen along with the bottle.

"Wow, a wine glass," she said, taking it from him.

"This is a classy place," he said, smiling.

She was touched by his having gone to the trouble to buy a wine glass for her, and though it was a small thing, it gave her another reason to believe the relationship was serious for him. An hour later finding clean sheets on the bed gave her another reason. From the absence of his roommate, the wine glass, and the clean sheets, she knew he had planned to make love with her, but she also knew he had wanted to make things nice for her. And without a doubt it was nicer on a bed than on a sofa.

On Friday when she met Gabby at O'Malley's she felt as if they hadn't seen each other for years, though it had only been a week. They were celebrating the end of Gabby's first semester as a graduate student when Danny arrived and stopped and touched Paola gently on the shoulder before joining his group at the round table.

"It's serious, isn't it," Gabby said.

"How can you tell?"

"I can tell by looking at you."

"Well, I hope my mother can't tell by looking at me."

"You haven't told her you have a boyfriend?"

"I told her it wasn't serious. But it is now."

"So you've had time with him alone?"

"Yeah. I went to his place, and he was *so sweet.*"

Gabby put an arm around her, saying: "I'm glad for you."

"Thanks. But I need to do something so I don't get pregnant."

"I can help you," Gabby said, reaching for her pocketbook. She took out a notepad and a pen and wrote on the top piece of paper. "This is my doctor."

"Is it a man or a woman?"

"A woman. I wouldn't want a man to examine me. I got her from my sister."

Gabby had an older sister whose experience made her a valuable resource. Paola would have liked to have an older sister. In most situations, especially this one, it wasn't useful having older brothers.

"Here," Gabby said, handing her the piece of paper. "Her office is across from St. John's Hospital, the third building if you're going north."

Looking at the doctor's name, Paola was glad that it was Italian.

Counting from her last period, she believed it was still safe to have sex, but she was approaching the time of fertility, so she made an appointment for Tuesday morning and told her father she would be late for work, giving as a reason that she had to do something for a friend. It wasn't a complete lie because birth control was also for Danny.

While she was having the examination she was glad that the

doctor was a woman, and in her mind she thanked Gabby.

She got the pills from the pharmacy on the subfloor of the medical building and buried them in her pocketbook, where she decided to keep them because her mother had no reason to go there. She took her first pill at the water-cooler of the office and followed Benny out to their truck, feeling as if she had passed another milestone.

Their first job was in a house on North Broadway where a man who thought he was an electrician had tried to rewire his circuit box. While Benny straightened out the mess, Paola stood between the box and the man, who wanted to see what Benny was doing, probably so he could fix it himself.

Though she hadn't consciously worried about getting pregnant while making love with Danny the first two times, not having to worry about it made a difference when she made love with him the next time.

Two days before Christmas, when they went to his apartment there was a shopping bag from Lord & Taylor on the sofa. Danny walked over and picked it up and handed it to her, saying: "This is for you."

Surprised, she said: "But I didn't get anything for you."

"You don't have to. And anyway, what could you get for me?"

It was hard to think of anything other than a piece of furniture for his apartment, and that wouldn't have been appropriate.

"You can put it under the tree," he said, "and open it on Christmas."

"Okay," she said, knowing that if she did, it would raise a lot of questions.

She gave him a big hug, still holding the bag by its handles, and it didn't take them long to relocate to the bedroom.

When she got home that night she decided not to wait until Christmas. In the privacy of her bedroom she lifted a box out of the bag and opened the box and parted the tissue paper and saw a sweater, a lovely shade of blue. She took off the sweater she was wearing and tried on his present and looked at herself in the mirror over her chest of drawers. The sweater fit her perfectly, and it suited her perfectly. She couldn't have picked a better one herself.

After some deliberation she wore the sweater for the family celebration on Christmas Eve, which followed the tradition of the Feast of Seven Fishes. There were eight people at the table: her grandmother, her mother and father, her two brothers, and her Uncle Rocco and Aunt Emilia, whose only son, her cousin Bobby, was spending Christmas with his wife's family in Pasadena. Working in the kitchen for the past few days, her grandmother and her mother had prepared an antipasto of olives, artichokes, mushrooms, mussels, shrimp, and salt cod salad, followed by a pasta course of eggplant lasagna, and then as main courses braised octopus, clams in white sauce, squid in tomato sauce, and roasted bass, with broccoli rabe and fennel as vegetables. Paola helped her mother carry the food from the kitchen to the table, and when they were seated, her grandmother said grace.

Before taking a bite of food her grandmother stared across the table and said: "Paola, that's a lovely sweater. Did someone give it to you?"

"Yeah. My boyfriend gave to me."

"You have a boyfriend?" her father asked as if it was a complete surprise.

"Yeah, I do." She looked around the table, ready for questions.

"What's his name?" her aunt asked.

"Danny," she said tentatively.

"He's Irish," her mother said, explaining the name.

"Well, if he gave you that sweater for Christmas," her aunt said, "he must be serious. It looks expensive. Where did he buy it?"

"At Lord & Taylor," Paola said.

Her aunt nodded as if that confirmed her assessment of its monetary value.

"Are you serious about this guy?" her father asked her.

"Yeah, I am."

"Then we gotta meet him."

Paola had expected this, so she wasn't surprised. In fact, she welcomed the suggestion. "Okay. We can go to dinner at D & V."

That ended the questions, at least for now, and while they continued feasting they talked about other things.

When she had finished helping her mother clean up the kitchen she retreated to her bedroom, where she looked at herself in the mirror again. She appreciated the sweater not only as a means by which Danny had made a commitment to her, but also as a means by which she had made an announcement to her family.

She was wearing the sweater when she met Danny a few days later at O'Malley's. Approaching her, he gazed at the sweater and nodded, saying: "It looks good on you."

"Thanks. I love it."

"I have to admit, my sister Colleen helped me buy it. I wouldn't have known what size or what color or what do you call it—" He gestured, running his forefinger in an arc below his neck.

"Neckline."

"Yeah. I told her about the sweater you wore last Wednesday, and she knew what to look for. She knows clothes."

"Well, I wore it to our family dinner on Christmas Eve, and everyone noticed it. In fact, my parents want to meet you."

"Your parents want to meet me?" he said as if he didn't understand.

"Yeah, I've been going out with you for seven months, so they think it's time."

"Do they always want to meet the guys you go out with?"

"No, but I never went out with a guy this long."

"So they think we're serious?"

"Yeah. They do." She paused, searching his eyes, which seemed to be waiting for a cue from her. "And I think we are."

He smiled. "Yeah. I think we are."

"So I suggested that we have dinner at D & V. Is that okay?"

"Yeah, it's okay. When?"

"How about next Saturday? My parents never eat out on weeknights."

"Okay. I'm available then." She could tell he wanted to get this meeting over with as soon as possible, and she did too.

Of course her parents were available, and her mother reserved her favorite table at D & V for Saturday at six. Paola walked there with her parents, and Danny met them, arriving just as they were about to go into the restaurant, so she introduced him there on the sidewalk.

They sat down at the table near the window, with the men and the women opposite each other. The waitress, who was a niece of the owners, gave them menus and took their drink orders.

"We like the food here," her mother told Danny. "We hope you like it."

"I do like it," Danny said. "I've been here before."

"We've come here for dinner a few times," Paola said, hoping to convey the idea that they didn't just hang out at bars.

"Then you know what to order," her mother said.

"I always have the steak," Danny said.

"That's what our sons have."

"But maybe this time I'll have something different. What do you recommend?"

"If you like veal, you should order *scallopini*."

Perusing his menu, Danny said: "They have five different ways of cooking *scallopini*."

"Do you like mushrooms?"

"No, not really."

"You like the steak *pizzaiola?*"

"Oh, yeah."

"Then have the *scallopini pizzaiola*."

"Okay," Danny said, closing his menu.

"So you work at the electric company," her father said.

"Yeah, I'm a lineman," Danny said proudly.

"Then we have something in common—we both work with electric wire."

"Yeah. We work with different kinds of wire, but the same juice goes through them."

Her father nodded. "How long have you worked at that job?"

"About seven years. I was eighteen when I started there."

"It's a union job, right?"

"Right."

"Then unless something happens to you," her father said, "your job is secure."

"I don't expect anything to happen to me, but if it does, the company will take care of me."

"His father worked for the electric company," Paola said, "and he has a good pension."

"Was your father a lineman?"

"Yeah, for a long time, but then they moved him into a job managing work crews, so he was at a higher salary level when he retired."

The waitress brought their drinks: a glass of red wine for her father, white wine for her mother and her, and beer for Danny. She said: "I'll come back when you're ready to order."

Paola took a sip of wine, beginning to feel comfortable.

"Do your parents still live in Woodlawn?" her mother asked.

"Oh, yeah. They'd never leave their neighborhood."

"Did your parents grow up there?"

"My mother did, but my father came from Ireland when he was fifteen."

"And you have sisters?"

"Yeah, I have four sisters, three nieces, and two nephews."

"It must make your parents happy to have five grandchildren."

"They're really crazy about their grandchildren."

"Wait till they get older," Paola said, knowing how her own grandmother worried about her.

"Now, where did you go to high school?" her mother said, continuing the interrogation.

"Cardinal Spellman. My sisters went to St. Barnabas," he added as if he were anticipating the next question.

"Those are good schools. Did any of your sisters go to college?"

"One of my sisters went to Katharine Gibbs. She has a job as a secretary in Manhattan. The two who have children got married right out of high school, and the other joined the navy right out of high school."

"What does your sister do in the navy?"

"She works at a base in San Diego. I went there to see her, and I had a good time, but I wouldn't want to live in California. It's not for real people."

"So you plan to stay in New York?"

"Oh, yeah. In fact, I plan to stay in Yonkers."

Her mother nodded as if what she had heard so far was good.

"You like sports?" her father asked.

"Yeah, I like baseball and basketball. I played basketball in high school. I wasn't great, but I was good enough to make the team."

"Are you a Yankees fan?"

"Yeah. I'm from the Bronx," he added as an explanation.

"Well, last season could have been worse. At least we managed to get into the playoffs. And I like the new young players."

"You mean Jeter, Posada, Pettitte, and Rivera?"

"Yeah," her father said approvingly. "They'll give new life to the team."

"For a while I wondered about Rivera, but then he came back, and he looks like he'll be good in the bull pen."

"We need someone good in the bull pen to set up Wetteland."

"We also need more hitting, which I think we'll get from Jeter and Posada. And we still have Williams and O'Neill."

"We might get some more out of Boggs, but he's up there, so I'm pinning my hopes on the new young players."

"I like Jeter," Paola said.

"You and all the ladies," her father said.

Their food arrived, and they stopped talking for a while, and when they resumed talking it felt like the interrogation was over. Danny had said all the right things, and it wasn't because he was making an effort to win over her parents. It was because he was being himself.

As the winter passed, they saw each other more and more often, going from two nights a week to three and four and even five. In this progression they were aided by the fact that Ron's girlfriend's roommate had moved in with her boyfriend, and Ron had taken the roommate's place, so Danny had the apartment to himself.

Free as they were, they still had a limit on their relationship: they couldn't spend the night together. In fact, he couldn't take her home much later than midnight, or else it would be reported to her mother by her grandmother. Of course, while Nonna suspected the worst, it would never have occurred to her mother that Paola and Danny were making love, and it would have been completely unthinkable for her to spend the night with him.

By the middle of April they were talking about the possibility of getting married, and the more they talked about it, the more it made sense. If they were married, they could live together, and they wouldn't have to work around her parents.

One night in late May, when they went to his apartment, he handed her a small bag from a jewelry store. In the bag was a box, and in the box was a silver ring with a single diamond, exactly what she had always imagined as an engagement ring. Without hesitation she took the ring out of the box and handed it to him.

Understanding what she wanted, he gently put the ring on the left finger of her left hand.

"I love it," she said, feeling as if her joy was reflected by the diamond.

"Colleen helped me buy it," he said.

By now she knew that Colleen was the sister that he was closest to, the oldest one who had three children and lived in Yorktown.

They sealed their commitment with a long kiss.

At breakfast the next morning Paola showed the ring to her mother, who gave her a hug that validated the engagement. Her father didn't notice the ring, but when she pointed it out to him, he smiled and said: "He's a lucky guy."

She showed the ring to Gabby when they met at O'Malley's, and her friend gave her a hug that reinforced her mother's hug.

She showed the ring to the rest of her family when they gathered to celebrate Memorial Day with a cookout in the backyard, which except for a border of rose bushes was covered by reddish brown patio tiles. Her brothers were there, neither of them with a girlfriend, and her Uncle Rocco and Aunt Emilia were also there. And when she came out the back door with the bowl of ziti that her grandmother had made, she made sure that they saw the ring, though she had to flash her hand in front of her brothers to get them to notice it.

"It's a beautiful ring," her aunt said. "Where did he get it?"

"From Tiffany's," she said, though she knew he had gotten it somewhere else. He hadn't yet arrived, so she could embellish his buying it for her.

"Well, now we know he's serious."

The next step was for her to meet his family, so on Saturday he drove her over to Woodlawn and parked on a street that wasn't much different than the street where her parents lived, though his parents' house was for a single family.

His mother, who had wavy blond hair without a trace of gray, greeted them at the door with a friendly smile and led them into the living room, where his father was watching the Yankees game. The Yankees were at bat, with two men on base, and Jeter was up, so she was more than willing to wait until the play was over to be introduced.

When Jeter hit a single that drove in two runs she cheered along with the two men.

"You must be Paola," his father said with a lyrical brogue. He got up from the sofa and came to her with open arms. He was tall and lean with a full head of silver hair. Instead of shaking her hand, he took her gently by the shoulders and gazed at her, saying: "I'm really glad to meet you."

"She's a fan of Jeter," Danny told him.

"So am I. It's a different team from last year."

"Would you like something to drink?" his mother asked her.

She looked at Danny for a cue.

"We can have a drink at Monahan's." He had told her they were going to the neighborhood pub where his parents still went after church.

"We can have a drink here," his mother said. "We have white wine."

Guessing that his mother had bought the wine especially for her, Paola said: "I'll have some wine. I'll help you get it."

She followed his mother into the kitchen, leaving the two men with the baseball game. She stood by while his mother opened the refrigerator and took out a bottle. "I didn't know what kind of wine you like. Is Chardonnay okay?"

"It's fine. I hope you didn't go to any trouble."

His mother faced her, smiling. "I didn't. I had to go to the liquor store anyway."

"If you give me a corkscrew, I'll open it for you." Though her experience at using corkscrews was limited to the times at Danny's apartment when she opened bottles for herself, she figured it was more experience than his mother had.

His mother found a corkscrew in a drawer and handed it to her.

As she peeled the plastic from the top of the bottle his mother opened a cabinet and got three glasses, one of them for wine.

"We usually have a whiskey before dinner," his mother told her, "and then we have water during dinner. We used to drink beer, but it's too filling."

"I know what you mean. I started with beer, but now I drink wine. My parents drink wine, but not every day."

"So you're from Yonkers?"

"I was born and raised there."

His mother got a bottle out of another cabinet and set it on the counter next to the glasses. "Where did you go to school?"

"I went to St. Brigid through eighth grade, and then I went to Sacred Heart."

"But you didn't go to college."

"No, I didn't need college for the job I have."

After getting ice out of the refrigerator his mother said: "So you're an electrician."

"I'm not one yet. I'm still doing my apprenticeship."

"You work for your father?"

"Yeah. He has his own business."

"You like your job?"

"Oh, yeah. I like it a lot. I didn't want to be a secretary or a nurse or a teacher or a flight attendant."

"Good for you," his mother said, putting ice into the glasses. "I wish I'd dared to do something different."

"Well, you dared to have five children."

His mother laughed affectionately. "Paola, I love you. My only son, who was spoiled by his sisters, is lucky to have you."

They had dinner at Monahan's, where everyone seemed to know Danny and his parents. Between bits of conversation his father regaled them with stories that made them all laugh, even though Danny and his mother must have heard them before. Since Paola hadn't heard them before, she laughed harder than they did, and seeing how well his father told stories, she knew where Danny's gift had come from.

They decided to have the wedding in September. It had to be at St. Brigid, where she had been baptized and confirmed, and luckily there was a time available toward the end of the month. They met with the priest, Father Paul, who dutifully questioned them about their commitment to the sacrament of marriage and told them that if they had any doubts, even at the last minute, they could always call it off. As an example, he cited a couple who had called off their wedding while people were already sitting in the church, waiting for the ceremony to begin.

Paola asked Gabby to be her maid of honor, and Danny asked Ron to be his best man. They agreed to limit the wedding party to their parents and these two friends, and they arranged to have the reception at the Polish Center, which did a lot of wedding receptions. She didn't see how there could be more than fifty people on the invitation list, but before they knew it there were more than a hundred, most of them family.

With the help of her mother and Colleen, who knew how to buy things for her, she got her dress at Lord & Taylor. On her wedding day she looked like the bride she had dreamed of, and Danny looked like the groom she had dreamed of. She was so happy, she wished the ceremony had lasted longer.

They had a good time at the reception, and with a joyous send-off from their families and friends they departed for their honeymoon. They stayed at an inn in Stonington, Connecticut, a two-and-a-half-hour drive from Yonkers. After three days of eating mostly clams and scallops and lobsters they found an Irish pub in nearby Mystic, where they felt at home.

FIVE

THEIR PLAN WAS to live in Danny's apartment for a few years and save enough money for a down payment on a house. They had a good deal on the rent, and though they didn't find much use for the extra bedroom, it was good to have, especially when someone needed a place to crash for the night. They still spent a few evenings a week at O'Malley's, and Paola still met Gabby there on Fridays, staying in touch with her friend, while Danny entertained his friends at the round table. But to save money they ate at home more often now with Paola cooking and acquiring a repertoire of Italian dishes from her mother and her grandmother.

Growing up, Paola had always gone to Sunday mass with her family, and she convinced Danny to go with her. Since they were no longer staying out late on Saturday night, he had no excuse for not being able to get up in time for the noon mass at St. Brigid, and if for no other reason, he went along with her to please her parents, whom they joined in the pew where her family had always sat.

They had two happy years living together and getting to know each other. The more she got to know Danny, the more she loved him and the happier she was. And she could feel that the same thing was happening to him.

Shortly after their second anniversary Colleen asked them if they could spend a weekend at her house in Yorktown babysitting her children, who were five, seven and nine, because she and her husband had to go to Boston for the wedding of his cousin. Having no plans for that weekend and feeling they owed a lot to Colleen, they readily accepted. And they had so much fun with the children, tossing a large inflated ball around the backyard and swimming in the pool and walking in the woods and playing games and eating hotdogs, that they could talk about nothing else on the way home.

"It was so much fun," Paola said. "It made me want to have our own kids."

"It made me feel the same way," Danny said with his hands steady on the wheel of the car and his eyes straight ahead. "Though having kids isn't always fun."

"I know. But whatever happens, it's rewarding. At least that's what my mother says."

"My mother says that too. But I don't feel any pressure from her. She already has five grandchildren."

"I don't feel any pressure from my mother. My brothers feel pressure from her."

"You mean to get married."

"Well, my mother doesn't want them to have kids without being married."

Danny laughed. "So if we don't feel any pressure from our mothers to have kids, we can make our own decision to have them. You think we're ready?"

"I think we're ready."

"Then let's have kids."

That night she went off the pill, and it didn't take her long to conceive. By the end of the year she was two months pregnant, and by early February there were looking for a house with the help of an agent they knew from O'Malley's.

Paola wanted to live close enough to her parents so that they could help her but not so close that they could interfere with her, so they looked for a house on the other side of Roberts Avenue, about a half mile from her parents. And they finally found a house on Bellevue Place, a perfect house with three bedrooms, one full bathroom, and a powder room.

"We'll have enough bedrooms," Danny said as they stood in one of them. "If we have three kids, and if two of them are boys or girls, they can double up."

"My brothers doubled up," she said.

"My sisters did too. We had four bedrooms."

"But what if all three of them are girls? Or boys?"

"Then the oldest can have their own bedroom."

With a little financial help from their parents they had enough for the down payment, and in late April they closed on the house. They moved the furniture from Danny's apartment, and they bought furniture for their bedroom, the baby's room, the living room, and the dining room.

The third bedroom was still unfurnished in early July when Briana arrived. Paola's pregnancy had seemed to go well, but there were complications with her delivery, and the doctor told her it almost killed her. It left her with the choice of risking her life for a future child or preserving her life for the present child, so the unfurnished bedroom ended up being used as a storeroom. Still, her gratitude for having Briana far outweighed her regret for not being able to have more children, and they became a tight family of three.

Paola had taken an indefinite maternity leave so she could be with her baby, and during that time her mother helped her and taught her things she might have learned only by trial and error. She didn't go out except to shop for groceries and other essentials, and when she did, she left the baby with her mother. When she and Danny needed a night out her mother and father came to their house and stayed with the baby.

Briana grew into a happy, active child, and early on she revealed a gift for entertaining people, which she must have gotten from her father. Watching the two of them exchange stories, Paola felt doubly blessed.

Despite being an only child, Briana didn't show any signs of being spoiled. In fact, she showed a lot of concern for other people, and she was only ten when she announced her intention of becoming a nurse. She had evidently gotten the idea from visiting St. John's Hospital while her great-grandmother was being treated there for a broken hip.

She went to elementary school at St. Brigid and then she started high school at Sacred Heart. She was doing well and getting good grades when the accident happened.

By then Paola had turned forty, and she was running the family business. Her father had nominally retired, but he still went to the office almost every day for a few hours, just to make sure that everything was all right. Since his sons had no interest in the business, with their approval he transferred full ownership to his daughter.

In the meantime, with her father's encouragement, Paola had completed a bachelor's degree in business administration from St. Catherine. It took her eight years, with one evening course in the classroom and one online course during the fall and spring, and one online course during the summer. She started the program the year Briana started elementary school at St. Brigid, and she finished it the year her daughter graduated from St. Brigid. So that spring they had two graduations, mother and daughter.

Danny was still working as a lineman. Though the company had given him opportunities for management positions, he turned them down because he still loved his job and the last thing in the world he wanted to do was sit at a desk behind a computer.

It happened in the early spring while Paola was on a job in Crestwood, wiring a new kitchen with Nelson, a young man whom she had mentored through the process of getting licensed as an electrician. Nelson was an immigrant from the Dominican Republic who had come to Yonkers with his family at the age of nine. He had gone to public schools in Yonkers, and he spoke perfect English, though he still had a slight accent that identified him as a Latino. He was a good worker, and Paola could easily imagine him assuming greater responsibilities.

By then everyone had cell phones, and she was installing an outlet when she felt a vibration in her pocket. Since she had given her cell phone number only to members of her family, a few friends, and the company's office, she was reasonably sure it wasn't a marketing call, so she took out her phone and saw it was from Danny.

"Hello?" she said, wondering why he was calling her.

"Mrs. O'Dwyer?" said a male voice. "This is Joe Donahue. I'm using Danny's phone because I don't know how else to reach you."

"What happened?" she asked, feeling as if the bottom had fallen out of her stomach.

"He had an accident. It didn't kill him, but it hurt him seriously. He's at St. John's Hospital, and I'm here with him."

"What floor are you on?"

"The eighth."

"Okay. I'll be there in a few minutes. Nelson," she said while she put away her phone, "I gotta go. When you finish here, call the office and ask them to pick you up."

"I hope everything's all right," he said, looking concerned.

"Yeah, I hope so," she said without pausing to collect her tools. She knew he would collect them for her. And without another word she raced out of the house to her truck.

It took her more than a few minutes to get to the hospital and find a place for her truck in the visitors parking area. She hurried to the main entrance and went to the elevator and pressed the button for the eighth floor, before pressing the button for another floor as requested by a woman in the back of the elevator.

On the eighth floor she went to the nurses station and told a woman who was gazing at a computer screen: "I'm here to see a patient. His name is Danny O'Dwyer."

"Who are you?"

"I'm his wife."

"I think he's still in surgery."

"Can you tell me what happened to him?"

"That gentleman can tell you," the nurse said, pointing to a man who was sitting in a plastic chair at the opposite side of the hall.

Joe was sitting with his head bowed as if he was praying.

"Joe?" she said, approaching him.

He looked up, blinking.

"I'm Danny's wife."

He lifted himself from the chair, saying: "Mrs. O'Dwyer, I'm so sorry."

"You can call me Paola. Tell me what happened."

He heaved his shoulders, taking a deep breath. "We were out on a job together. I was in the truck, and Danny was up in the bucket—"

Paola waited anxiously for him to continue.

"I was watching him, and all of a sudden the bucket tipped over and dumped him out."

"Where did he land?"

"He landed on the pavement. The impact was mostly on his right shoulder. But he also hit his head, and it knocked him out. I called EMS, and they came right away. I also called the office, which found another lineman to finish the job, and I drove the work crew manager's car here."

"Did you see him after they brought him here?"

"No, he went right into surgery. I'm waiting to hear from them."

"How long ago did he go into surgery?"

Joe checked his watch. "It's almost two hours ago."

"I'll be right back," she told him, turning. She went over to the nurses station and called to the woman she had talked with before. "Can you tell me anything about his condition?"

"I'm sorry. I can't. They took him directly from the ER to the OR, so all I know is, we were told to have a bed for him."

"Well, please let me know as soon as you hear anything."

"I will. If you want to, you can wait in the lounge at the end of the hall."

She went back to Joe and persuaded him to go to the lounge with her. As they walked down the hall she asked: "How could the bucket tip over?"

"I don't know. It just did."

"Then there must have been something wrong with it."

"They're supposed to inspect it."

"They evidently didn't."

"If they didn't, then it's the company's fault."

She understood the implication. If it was simply an accident, the company would give him compensation, but if the company had been negligent, they would have to give him more compensation. But she didn't care about compensation. She only wanted him to be all right.

The lounge had windows with a view of the river that included the George Washington Bridge and the skyline of Manhattan. There were several chairs and a coffee table with a scattering of random magazines. An old man who looked asleep was occupying one of the chairs, and the others were empty.

Paola and Joe sat down to wait. For a long time neither of them spoke, and in the silence Paola prayed. She didn't pray often, not wanting to bother God with minor problems but saving the recourse of prayer for occasions when she really needed help. And now, based on what she knew about the situation, she really needed help.

"How long have you been married?" Joe asked, interrupting the silence.

"Eighteen years."

"Do you have kids?"

"We have one. She's fifteen." She had no idea how long Joe and Danny had worked together, but if they had been women, information about their husbands, kids, and parents would have been shared within a few hours.

"Does your daughter know what happened?"

"No. She's at school now. And I don't want to tell her until I know what happened."

"You know what happened. The bucket tipped over and dumped him out."

"I meant until I know how he is. I don't want to scare her."

They had fallen into another silence when a doctor appeared, still in his scrubs.

"Are you Mrs. O'Dwyer?" he asked her.

"Yeah," she said, bracing herself.

"Your husband's in the recovery room. The good news is, we managed to limit the damage to his nervous system, so he won't be paralyzed. But there's a lot of damage in his right shoulder and his right arm, so he'll need surgery later for that."

"He landed on his right shoulder," Joe said.

"You saw the accident?" the doctor asked him.

"Yeah. I saw it. He was in a cherry picker, and all of a sudden the bucket tipped over and dumped him out."

"How high up was he?"

"About thirty feet."

The doctor nodded. "Well, he's damn lucky. It didn't kill him, and it didn't leave him paralyzed. But he won't be able to work as a lineman anymore."

"When can I see him?" Paola asked.

"In an hour or so. We need to keep him in the recovery room for a while."

When the doctor had left she gave thanks for Danny not being killed or paralyzed, but she was concerned by the doctor's opinion that he wouldn't be able to work as a lineman anymore. And she prayed that the doctor was wrong.

As she waited for Danny to get out of the recovery room she called her parents' house. She didn't know if Briana would be at home or at a friend's house, and anyway she wanted to talk with her mother first, not only to get some moral support but also to get some guidance.

She related to her mother what Joe had told her, and what the doctor had told her, though she didn't repeat the doctor's opinion that Danny wouldn't be able to work as a lineman anymore. Her mother agreed with her decision not to call Briana until after she saw Danny and made her own assessment of things. She asked her mother to tell her father what had happened and to be available later to drive Briana to the hospital.

Though she wanted to put off telling his parents so that she would have some time alone with Danny before they got involved, she decided that it wouldn't be right to keep them in the dark, so she called his parents' house and talked with his mother, who agreed to tell his father and to wait until she heard back from Paola before they came to the hospital.

After making these calls she didn't have to wait much longer for Danny to be released from recovery and transferred to a room.

Joe went with her, and they found him in a room with two beds, one of them empty. He was propped up in a reclining position, still in a daze, though his drowsy eyes brightened with recognition of his wife and his coworker.

"How are you doing?" Paola asked him.

"Okay," he said faintly.

"Are you in pain?"

"No. They gave me a drug."

"Then you're zoned out," Joe said.

"I guess I am." He closed his eyes and opened them. "I was trying to remember exactly what happened."

"You were in the bucket, and it tipped over."

"It just tipped over?"

"Yeah, it did. And it dumped you out. You landed on the pavement."

Danny made a face as if he could imagine how that had felt. "Well, I must have landed on my shoulder."

"You did. You're lucky you didn't land on your head."

"I hit my head. I can tell from how it feels. But I must have pulled it out of the way."

While they were talking Paola moved around the bed so that she could take his left hand and hold it. His hand was cool, as if it had been in a refrigerator.

He turned his head to her. "Did the doctor tell you how I am?"

"He told us you won't be paralyzed," she said, "but you'll need more surgery for the damage to your shoulder and your arm."

"How bad is the damage?"

"It's bad enough so you'll need more surgery, but until they do it, they really won't know."

"Yeah, that's what he told us," Joe said.

"Shit," Danny said, loading the word with emotion. "Did it have to be my *right* arm?"

"You could have been killed or paralyzed," she reminded him.

"I know, but I wasn't, so don't tell me I'm lucky."

"You *are* lucky," Paola insisted. "And let's pray that with more surgery your shoulder and your arm will be fine."

"You do the praying," he told her.

Attributing this remark to the fact that he was on a drug and didn't have full possession of his faculties, she didn't think much about it. She let go of his hand and called Briana, who was at a friend's house. She told Briana that her father was in the hospital, he was doing fine, and her grandparents would bring her there. Then she called her parents and told them where Briana was so they could pick her up. And finally she called Danny's mother to give her an update.

Meanwhile, a nurse came in and did his vitals. She was a nice girl, and Danny kidded her about the color of her scrubs. He also kidded Joe about leaving the work crew manager's car in the visitors parking area, where it could fall into the wrong hands.

A half hour later Paola's parents arrived with Briana, who rushed to her father and threw her arms around him, pressing her face against his chest.

"Be careful of my shoulder," Danny told her.

Briana raised her head, asking: "What happened to your shoulder?"

"I landed on it falling from a bucket."

"You fell from a bucket? How did that happen?"

"I thought I was an eagle, and when I stretched my wings to fly, I dropped like a stone."

"You didn't," Briana said, giggling.

"I did. I thought the bucket was my nest."

"Does your shoulder hurt?"

"It doesn't now, but it will when the painkiller wears off."

"Will your shoulder be all right?"

"It'll be fine," Danny said confidently. "They just need to do more work on it."

"Can I get you something to drink?" Briana asked, assuming the role of nursing assistant.

"Yeah, you can get me a bottle of Bud."

"You're not allowed to drink beer in a hospital," Briana said, turning to her mother and her grandmother for confirmation.

"He can't drink beer here," Paola said. "But he can drink water."

"I don't need water," Danny said. "They're pumping water into me through this tube."

"When they let you out, we can go to O'Malley's."

"When are they going to let me out?"

"I don't know. I think you'll be here for a few days."

At that moment Danny's parents arrived, and with the room getting crowded, Paola went out into the hall with her father.

"He's kidding about it," her father said. "But how bad is it?"

Paola sighed. "The doctor said he wouldn't be able to work as a lineman anymore."

"Well, I hope the doctor's wrong. Danny loves that job."

"It's the only job he ever wanted."

"But he seems in good spirits."

"I didn't tell him what the doctor said."

"Shouldn't you tell him?"

"I don't want to demoralize him. And the doctor could be wrong."

"Yeah." Her father put a hand on her shoulder. "I guess we won't know until after they do more work on him."

From the room came a peal of laughter. Someone, either Danny or his father or Briana, must have told a story. She hoped it was Danny.

Three days later they released him from the hospital. Briana got an excused absence from school, and she was there to help her father get into the car, and out of it, and into the house, and into a chair in the living room, where he could watch television. He couldn't have the restorative surgery for at least two months, but he would have physical therapy twice a week. The company put him on a medical leave until after the surgery. So for the next two months he had nothing to do but physical therapy.

Since Briana wasn't old enough to drive, Paola had to take Danny to therapy, which he had at the branch of St. John's in Dobbs Ferry. It was on the lower floor in the orthopedics department, one of whose doctors took over Danny's case from the doctor who had done the emergency surgery. This doctor prescribed the therapy, and he examined Danny every two weeks to monitor his progress. He was a man of few words, and in response to Paola's repeated questions, he would only say that

Danny was doing as expected, but he never revealed what was expected. He left her simply hoping for the best.

On the days when Danny had physical therapy, Paola took the afternoon off from work, and her father helped her manage the business. In the morning she went to the office and reviewed jobs with her father before she left to take Danny to therapy. And while she was waiting for Danny she used her cell phone to keep track of what was happening on the jobs.

Briana helped her with Danny at home. She not only got him whatever he needed, but she also kept him company. The main thing they did together was watch movies on television, most of them violent action movies, but Paola didn't object to them because she understood Danny's need to kill time. They were both waiting anxiously for the restorative surgery.

After several weeks of this routine she had a chance to vent her feelings with Gabby, whom she met on a Friday at O'Malley's. By then her friend was a psychologist for the Yonkers public school system, and since they had so many obligations as wives and mothers, they no longer met every Friday for drinks but they still met at least once a month.

"What I hate," she told Gabby, "is the uncertainty. If they could just tell us what to expect, we could prepare for it. But all we can do now is wait and hope."

"Well, maybe you should prepare for the worst," Gabby said. "If it happens, you'll be ready for it. If it doesn't happen, you'll feel blessed."

"That's what my mother tells me."

"Yeah. I learned that from *my* mother."

"But if I did that, I'd be alone. Danny and Briana are expecting the surgery to cure him."

"If they want a miracle they should go to Lourdes."

"They don't want a miracle, they expect one. It's like they feel entitled to one."

"But you don't feel entitled to one."

"No. I mean, someone in the family has to face reality."

"It sounds like you don't expect the surgery to cure Danny."

"I don't know what to expect. The doctor won't tell me. And I keep thinking about what that doctor at the hospital said."

"If he's not an orthopedist," Gabby said, "he probably doesn't know what to expect."

"He probably doesn't," Paola agreed. "But he must have seen a lot of cases."

After a silence Gabby asked: "How old is Danny?"

"He's forty-four."

"Then even without this accident he shouldn't be a lineman anymore. At his age he should be a manager."

"They offer him positions as a manager. But he keeps saying he doesn't want to sit at a desk behind a computer."

"He could manage work crews out in the field. He wouldn't have to sit at a desk."

"Well, maybe that's what he should do," she said hopefully.

But when she broached the idea to Danny he refused to consider it. He expected to be cured by the surgery and to be given his old job as if nothing had happened.

They had to wait until September for the surgery. The orthopedist wanted to give Danny ample time to recover from his injury, and he rejected any possibility of doing the operation sooner. In the meantime Danny was in a lot of pain, so he continued taking painkillers.

A few weeks after the accident Paola drove him to the office of the electric company, where she sat in a waiting area while he had a meeting with the human resource department. They gave some options for using his time until the surgery. These options didn't include working at his usual job, and even Danny admitted that in his present condition he couldn't have done it. He chose the least unattractive option, which was taking workshops on various topics ranging from safety to teamwork. The workshops were boring, except for the one on teamwork, the instructor of which had worked on crews for the company and was good at telling stories from his experience.

The time passed slowly, but the date of the surgery finally

arrived. They were going to do a shoulder replacement, which the doctor said was the only way to relieve the pain and give Danny a chance of recovering the use of his shoulder. But he warned them that he wasn't likely to recover more than about two-thirds of normal shoulder motion, which raised the question of whether that would be enough for Danny to resume his job.

Briana took a day off from school so that she could sit in the waiting room with her mother while they did the procedure. After an hour she gave up playing on her phone and read an old *National Geographic*, which had an article about polar bears. Paola tried to read a novel that Gabby had liked, but it barely distracted her from what was happening in the operating room. The surgery was taking so long, she wondered if they had encountered a problem. But finally, after more than two hours, the doctor emerged and told her it had gone well.

About an hour later they went to the room where Danny had been moved to, and they found him sitting up in bed with a huge bandage on his right shoulder. He greeted them with a wan smile, offering them the palm of his left hand for a low five.

"The doctor said it went well," Paola said, gently slapping his hand.

"Yeah, that's what he said. Do we know what that means?"

"It means the operation was successful."

He nodded. "Yeah. Well, I hope it was. I don't want any more hospitals."

By then Briana had taken her turn slapping his hand and was standing by, ready to help him.

"Could you get me a beer?" Danny asked her.

"Sure," Briana said, going along with him. "A bottle of Bud?"

"What else? I never drink imported beers."

From a pitcher on the table next to the bed, Briana poured him a glass of water, and the two of them pretended it was beer.

They kept him in the hospital for two days after the surgery. While he was still there they started the process of rehabilitation with a therapist moving his arm for him. They gave him an exercise program to follow when he went home, and the therapist showed him how to use a pulley device to move his arm.

Before he left the hospital they gave him a printed rehab schedule. It had six weeks of very limited activity during which he wasn't allowed to use his shoulder muscles. He was supposed to use the pulley to move his arm four or five times a day. There were prescribed exercises that included rotating his arm and elevating his shoulder. He had to wear a sling at night. And he wasn't supposed to lift anything heavier than a cup of coffee.

After six weeks he could start doing exercises that used his shoulder muscles, working with a therapist to stretch the soft tissues around the shoulder. This stage of the rehab would last until about three months after surgery, and then he would begin more intensive training.

So, as long as there were no complications, it would be at least three months before he could expect to regain normal functions of his shoulder.

"Three months?" he said, sitting in his assigned chair in the living room. "They say I can't go back to my job until December?"

"That's when you can begin more intensive training, so the whole process is going to take longer than three months."

"How much longer?"

"I don't know. They don't say. But it might take four months."

"Until January?" He shook his head. "I can't sit around that long doing nothing."

"You won't be doing nothing. You'll be doing rehab."

"That doesn't occupy the whole day."

"Well, the company will find something for you to do. They're paying your full salary."

"They owe it to me. I've worked there for twenty-six years. And it's their fault the bucket tipped over."

Two weeks later she drove him to the electric company, and again she sat in a waiting area while he met with the human resource department. When he emerged from the meeting he didn't look happy, but he wouldn't tell her what had happened until they were in the car.

"So what did they say?" she asked after they had driven for a while in silence.

"They want me to take a management training course," he said as if it was some kind of punishment.

"How long would it take?"

"About three months."

"Well, that's perfect. It would give you something to do until you finish rehab."

"But I don't want to be a manager."

"Why not? Your father eventually became a manager. And if he did it, why won't you?"

"I'm not him," Danny said obstinately.

"I know you're not him. I was giving him as an example."

"The only thing my father liked about being a manager was getting a higher salary."

"That's probably the only thing most people like about being a manager."

"Then why should I be a manager when I can do a job I love?"

"What if you can't do that job?"

"You mean you don't believe I can?"

"I believe you can, but I don't *know* you can, and I want to be prepared for the worst."

He was silent for a while, and then he said: "Well, I'll take this training course. I gotta do something for the next three months. But I don't want to be a manager."

The course included training on computers, which he had never used before, and so that he could practice the lessons at home they bought a laptop and a worktable with a height where he wouldn't strain his shoulder using the keyboard. They set the table in the spare bedroom after clearing a space among the items being stored there, and gradually they converted the room into an office for him.

Paola had learned to use computers in the business program at St. Catherine, but she was far from being an expert, and she let the office manager of the family business do almost everything that had to be done on a computer. So when Danny had questions or problems he relied on Briana, who like most members of her generation had grown up with computers. Whenever Paola heard him yelling at the computer she knew that Briana would run to help him, though if Briana wasn't home, Paola had to help him. Most of the time she was able to help him, but when she wasn't, then he always made her feel it was her fault that the computer wouldn't do what he wanted it to do. Aware of his pain and frustration, she didn't blame him for making her feel this way, and she didn't object to his treatment of her. She felt that somehow it *was* her fault.

Again, the time passed slowly. The rehab continued, and the doctor kept saying it was going well. By early May the stage of intensive training was over, and it was time for Danny to be evaluated to determine if he could resume his job as a lineman. Before sending his report to the company the doctor met with them in his office, and though his face didn't reveal anything, as soon as they sat down in front of him Paola sensed that he wasn't going to tell them what they wanted to hear.

Addressing Danny, the doctor said: "You've recovered a little more than half the normal functions of your shoulder, and if you keep doing the exercises, you should recover more. But I don't know if you've recovered enough to resume your job as a lineman. The company has to make that decision."

"Are you making a recommendation?" Danny asked.

"No. I'm reporting the facts, which mainly concern the range of motion in your shoulder and your arm."

"So the company will decide if I can do the job?"

"Right. And since you must know what that job requires, you shouldn't get your hopes up."

He did get his hopes up, and when the company made its decision he was devastated. He burst out of the human resource department, yelling: "I'm going to sue those motherfuckers. I'm going to sue them."

SIX

AFTER A LONG discussion, in which Danny refused to change his position, he agreed to ask his father for advice. He wanted Paola and his mother present at the conversation, so the next day they met after dinner in the living room of his parents' house. Since his father had worked more than forty years for the electric company and always said positive things about it, Paola hoped he would influence Danny.

"Now, what did they get from the doctor?" his father asked after hearing about the company's decision not to allow Danny to continue working as a lineman.

"They got a report on my shoulder and my arm."

"And what did the report say?"

"It said I had almost normal motion in my shoulder and my arm."

"It said you have a little more than half the normal motion," Paola said.

Danny looked at her as if he didn't understand why she had corrected his version.

"If you want your father's advice," she said, "you have to tell him the truth. And the truth is, you have a little more than half the normal motion in your shoulder and your arm."

"Is that what the report says?" his father asked Danny.

Danny shrugged. "Yeah, that's what it says. But I'm getting better every day."

"If you regain the normal motion, you can ask them to review your case. But if you have only a little more than half the normal motion, then I don't see how you can do the job."

"I know I can do it."

"Well, they don't think you can. And it's their decision, not yours."

"So I'm supposed to let them fuck me?"

"They're not fucking you. They're offering you another job, which they'll train you for."

"I don't want another job. I want my old job."

"They don't want you to do that job," his father said. "And they have good reasons. You could get hurt, and the guys working with you could get hurt."

"But this isn't fair. It's their fault I had the accident, and they should do something to make things right."

"Explain to me again how it's their fault you had the accident," his father said, sitting forward in the easy chair with his arms resting on his knees.

"The equipment was faulty. It hadn't been inspected. And that's their fault. It wasn't my job to inspect the equipment."

"Did you test it?"

"Yeah, I tested it," Danny said.

His father frowned. "And while you were up there, the bucket tipped over?"

"Yeah, it tipped over."

"If that's what happened, you have a case. But suing them isn't the way to go. You should ask them for compensation."

"You haven't done that, have you?" Paola said.

"No, I've only asked them for my old job."

"Then ask them for compensation and take the job they're offering you."

"I don't want to sit at a desk behind a computer. I hate computers," Danny added vehemently.

"They're offering you a desk job?"

"That's what it sounds like."

"Well, let me talk with them," his father said. "I still know some people at the company, and maybe I can get them to offer you a job managing work crews."

"That would be good," Paola said after waiting for Danny to say something.

"It might be good," he said. "I'd have to try it."

His mother, who had listened without intervening, finally said:

"Your father managed work crews, and he earned more money doing that than he did as a lineman."

"I don't care about the money. I want to have a job I love."

"You'll love managing work crews," his father assured him, leaning back in the easy chair. "I didn't think I'd love it, but I did."

A few days later he drove to the company for another meeting with the human resource department. Paola had agreed that he should drive himself as a way of demonstrating that he wasn't handicapped.

While he was there she worked in the office, discussing the monthly income and expenses with the bookkeeper. They were on the topic of payroll expenses when Danny called her and told her about the company's offer: a monthly payment as compensation for his injury and a job managing work crews. He wasn't happy about the job, but he hadn't turned it down. He had agreed to try it.

They gave him more training, and a month later they assigned him to a job on Nodine Hill. The job went well, and though he didn't love it, he thought he could live with it. The only thing he didn't like was the neighborhood, where everyone spoke Spanish. She didn't point out that this was the neighborhood where Nelson lived with his wife and their three children. And she didn't comment on his statement that if those people wanted to live in America, they should learn English, and if they didn't, they should go back where they had come from.

After several weeks of managing work crews he came home angry. Not wanting their daughter to hear whatever it was about, she sent Briana to get some things they needed at the pharmacy over on Palisade Avenue.

They were in the kitchen, and holding a bottle of beer that he had taken out of the refrigerator, Danny said: "Guess what those motherfuckers did."

Unable to guess, she could only ask: "What did they do?"

"They gave my old job to a Puerto Rican."

"How do you know?"

"I saw him get into a bucket truck with Joe."

"Well, they had to give the job to someone. Why do you care if he's Puerto Rican?"

"Don't you see?" He paused as if he expected her to see. "It wasn't about my shoulder and my arm. It was about increasing diversity."

"You actually think they wouldn't allow you to do your old job because they wanted to increase diversity?"

"Yeah, that's what I think."

Disturbed, she said: "I don't know where you got that idea. In fact, I never heard you talk that way about minorities."

"I never had a problem with them before. But now I have a problem with them."

"Danny, sweetheart," she pleaded with him. "They didn't take away your job because they wanted to give it to a Puerto Rican. They took away your job because you have a physical disability, so you couldn't do it."

"I could have done it."

"You couldn't have. Your father said you couldn't have."

"He only said he didn't see how I could do it. He never said I couldn't do it."

"Well, I also heard him say you shouldn't do it."

Danny took a swig of beer. "You know, I've thought about it, and I've decided that those motherfuckers aren't paying me enough compensation."

"We have enough income."

"Maybe we do have enough income, but I want them to pay me more compensation."

"Then ask them for more, but don't sue them. Your father said it's not the way to go."

"My father doesn't know. He had a different experience with the company."

"I don't know either, but I don't think you should sue them. You'd have to pay a lawyer, and you could lose."

"How could I lose?" Danny said. "I have a case against them."

"Before you decide anything," Paola advised him, "you should talk with my brother. He can tell you if you have a case, and it won't cost you anything."

"Okay. I'll talk with him. Ask him to meet us at O'Malley's tomorrow."

Anthony couldn't meet them the next day, but he could meet them two days later. He was now a partner at the law firm in White Plains where he had started right after passing the bar exam, he was married, he had two children, and he lived in Somers. He arrived a little late, for which he apologized, and they went to the table they had reserved.

As she sat down across from him Paola noticed that he had put on a little weight, which showed in his face, and that he was wearing an expensive suit. In terms of money, he seemed to have made the right decision to pursue a career as a lawyer instead of working at the family business. And she was happy for him.

"This place hasn't changed," he said. "The guys at the bar even look the same."

"Some of them are," Paola said, "though now they're older."

"We're all older. But you still look young."

"Thank you. It must be from working with electricity."

They waited until they had ordered food before getting into the matter. Danny related how the accident had happened and how it had affected him.

"You know, I don't do this kind of litigation," Anthony warned them, making a whoa gesture with his hands.

"I know you don't," Paola said. "But you can advise us."

"You want to know if I think you have a case?"

"Yeah. Before we hire a lawyer."

"Well, from what you said, you're claiming that the accident happened because the equipment was faulty. Do you have any evidence that it was faulty?"

"The bucket tipped over," Danny said.

"But you could have done something that caused it to tip over."

"I didn't do anything that caused it to tip over. I was doing my job as usual."

"Did they check the equipment after the accident?"

"I don't know. I assume they did."

"Then you need to know what they found out."

"So how could I get that information?"

"You could ask them. But if that information supported your case, they wouldn't give it to you. You'd have to subpoena their accident report."

"He'd need a lawyer to do that, wouldn't he?" Paola said.

"Yeah. He couldn't do that himself."

"If their accident report supported his case, would they pay him more compensation?"

"They might."

"Then he might not have to go beyond hiring a lawyer to subpoena the report?"

"He might not have to. But even if it supported his case, they might not pay him more compensation."

"Why wouldn't they?"

"They could drag the matter out for a long time," Anthony said. "They have deep pockets."

Hoping to get a definitive answer, Paola asked: "So would it be worth the risk for him to subpoena the report?"

Anthony grimaced. "If he takes legal action against them, he'll lose his job and he'll lose the compensation they're giving him. So it definitely wouldn't be worth the risk. As I said, they could drag the matter out for a long time, and even if he won his case, by then he could be ruined."

After this conversation Paola hoped that Danny would give up the idea of suing the company and accept what they had given him. But he kept going back to the idea, and he kept insisting that the company had taken away his job so they could give it to a Puerto Rican.

She shared her concerns with Gabby when they met that Friday at O'Malley's.

"It sounds like he's obsessed with the Puerto Rican," Gabby said.

"Things were going well," Paola said, "until he saw a Puerto Rican get into a bucket truck with a guy he used to work with. He actually thinks they took away his job so they could give it to a Puerto Rican. And I don't know where that idea came from."

"I don't remember him talking bad about minorities."

"He never did, and now when he talks bad about them I feel I don't know him."

Gabby considered. "Maybe it was deep inside him all along, and something brought it to the surface. He must need to blame someone for what happened to him."

"If he needs to blame someone, he should blame whoever failed to inspect the equipment."

"Does he know who was supposed to inspect it?"

"He doesn't talk about that issue. He just keeps talking about the Puerto Rican."

After taking a long sip of wine Gabby said: "Maybe one of his buddies was supposed to inspect the equipment."

"That's possible," Paola said, having seen his acts of loyalty to people. "You think he's protecting one of his buddies?"

"I think he's protecting someone."

"Well, I don't know who it could be, unless it's the guy who was working with him when the accident happened."

"Does Danny still hang out with him?"

"I don't think so. He hasn't mentioned that guy in a while."

"Then maybe you and Danny should talk with him and see what you can learn from him."

"Okay. But if Danny's protecting him, why would he want to sue the company? Wouldn't that uncover who was to blame for the accident?"

"Yeah, but it would get him off the hook. I mean, it would relieve him of the feeling that he has to protect someone."

"You think it's that complicated?"

"It's always that complicated," Gabby told her, "even with teenagers."

When she raised the question Danny insisted that he didn't know who was supposed to inspect the equipment, and when she suggested talking with Joe Donahue he insisted that Joe had nothing to do with the accident. But she finally talked him into it, arguing that it might give him valuable information for his suit against the company.

Joe lived in Woodlawn, so they met at Monahan's a few days later, taking a booth in a corner.

"How's your job going?" Joe asked after they had ordered their usual beers.

"It's going okay," Danny said. "But I'd rather be a lineman."

"I miss working with you. The guy I work with now is good, but he's not as good as you."

"What's his name?"

"His name is Jorge, but he calls himself George."

"Well, I don't care what he calls himself. I don't like having a spic take my job."

"He didn't take your job. They assigned him to it. They had to replace you."

"They didn't have to replace me," Danny insisted. "They *made a decision* to replace me."

"What's the difference?"

"It's a big difference. They made a decision to increase diversity at my expense."

"Come on, Danny," Joe said consolingly. "You're not the victim of a conspiracy. You're the victim of an accident."

"If anyone's to blame," Paola said, "it's whoever was supposed to inspect the equipment. Do you know who that was?"

"No, I don't know. Why does it matter?"

"It matters because Danny can get more compensation from the company if he can prove it was their fault."

Joe shook his head. "If I was Danny, I wouldn't pursue that."

"Why wouldn't you?"

"If he lost the case, he'd lose his job and the compensation they're already giving him."

"But if there's information in the accident report that supports his case, then he could win it."

"I wouldn't count on that," Joe said. "You think they'd put information in the report that could be used against them?"

"You mean they'd lie about what happened?"

"They wouldn't have to lie. They'd only have to leave out that information."

Paola considered. "Then it would be a waste of time and money to subpoena the report?"

"Yeah, it would be." Joe turned to Danny. "You're lucky you didn't break your neck. You're lucky you still have a job with them. And you're lucky you get compensation for your injury. So instead of suing the company, you should be thankful."

"I should be *thankful* for what they did to me?"

"They didn't do it to you, Danny. You did it to yourself."

"What the fuck do you mean by that?"

"You know what I mean," Joe said, looking at Danny in a way that excluded Paola.

On the way home she asked what Joe had meant, but Danny said he had no idea, and he dismissed Joe's advice, saying: "He was just taking the company line."

Ignoring the advice from his father, his brother-in-law, his former coworker, and his wife, Danny insisted on taking legal action against the company. Anthony found him a lawyer at a firm in White Plains that specialized in litigation, and Paola went with him to his first meeting with the lawyer, whose name was Jerry Ryan.

Jerry's office was in a new building on Main Street, and judging from the reception area and the number of lawyers employed by the firm, it was doing well. Jerry was a short man with ruddy skin and combative blue eyes. He met them in shirtsleeves, rolled up, and led them into a conference room, where he took the seat at the head of a table.

On a legal pad he took notes while Danny gave him a brief history of his experience with the company and told him what had happened to him.

"So you claim that the equipment was faulty," Jerry said, "and you want me to subpoena the accident report."

"Yeah, that's it," Danny said.

"Well, what if there's nothing in the report that supports your claim?"

"Then I guess I'm fucked."

"You're worse than fucked. You'll lose your job, and you'll lose your compensation."

"Could he apply to the government for disability?"

"Yeah, he could. But he might not get it, and even if he did, it wouldn't be as much as he's getting from the company."

"Then you don't think he should sue them?"

"No, I don't think he should. I think he should accept what they've offered him. I know what people think of our profession," Jerry added. "I mean that we'll do anything for money, but based on what you've told me, I don't want to take your money."

"But you don't know what's in the report," Danny argued.

"I don't know, but I can guess. It probably says the accident was caused by human error."

"Human error?"

"Yeah, human error. That's what those reports always say unless someone makes the company dig deeper."

"Isn't that your job? To make them dig deeper?"

"It's my job," Jerry said, "to take cases that I think I have a chance of winning."

"And you don't think you have a chance of winning this case?" Paola asked.

"Against the electric company? You realize how much money you'd have to spend?"

"But if we only asked you to subpoena the report, it would limit the cost."

Jerry cocked his head as if to get a better look at her. "It would limit the initial cost, but it wouldn't get him anywhere. He'd still have to litigate the case, and that would cost a bundle."

"What if he didn't go beyond getting the report?"

"What would be the purpose?"

"To get information that he could use in negotiating with the company. If the report supported his case, they couldn't ignore it."

"They sure as hell *could* ignore it," Jerry said, "and they could keep him dangling for years."

"But what would it cost us to get the report?"

"Without going further?"

"Yeah, without going further."

Jerry rolled his eyes upward and then replied: "Two thousand dollars plus expenses."

"What do you think?" she asked Danny.

"I think we should get the report," he said without hesitation.

"But taking legal action to get the report would also cost you what you're getting from the company in salary and compensation," Jerry reminded him. "It would give them cause for firing you."

"Yeah, I know."

Jerry sighed. "Well, why don't you guys sleep on it and let me know tomorrow what you decide. I want to make sure you understand the consequences."

As soon as they had left the building Paola said: "He doesn't want to take your case."

"I got that message," Danny said.

"He doesn't think you have a chance."

"Maybe he doesn't. But maybe he gets a lot of business from the electric company, and he doesn't want to hurt his relationship with them."

"Maybe, but I don't believe that. I believe he's honest."

"You believe everyone's honest," he muttered.

"No, I don't. I just had a good feeling about him."

"Well, let's sleep on it."

She didn't sleep on it. She lay awake most of the night worrying about it. She kept hearing what Joe had said, that Danny had done it to himself, and she wondered what Joe had meant by that. Had Danny somehow caused the accident? Had he done something reckless that had made the bucket tip over?

In the morning, while Briana was still sleeping, she confronted Danny with her questions. They were in the kitchen, having coffee.

"When we were talking with Joe," she said, "he said they didn't do it to you, you did it to yourself. What did he mean by that?"

"He didn't mean anything," Danny said crossly.

"Then why did he say it?"

"He was taking the company line."

She pulled herself together for the next question. "Did you do something that caused the accident?"

"Where did you get that idea?"

"From what he said. He said you did it to yourself."

"I didn't do anything that caused the accident," Danny said with his voice raised.

"Are you sure you didn't?"

He looked her directly in the eye, saying. "Yeah, I'm sure. I was doing my job."

"Well, I still don't think you should sue the company. Your father doesn't think you should, Anthony doesn't think you should, Joe doesn't think you should, and Jerry doesn't think you should. That's five of us who don't think you should sue the company."

"You mean it's five to one against me?"

"We're not against you. We're *for* you. We don't want you to get hurt even more."

"It's only money. Losing money won't hurt me."

"But losing your job will hurt you," she said, "and it'll also hurt your daughter. Think about Briana."

It looked as if she had finally reached him. He stopped arguing, and he left for work. But later, as she was doing a job in Irvington, he sent her a text message that said: "I'm going ahead with it. I have to."

It hurt her that he had made the decision without her, and it puzzled her that he felt he had to. Why did he have to? What need did he have to fulfill?

They waited almost three weeks to hear from Jerry, who had told Danny it would take a while for him to get the accident report. As things turned out, the report didn't have any information that supported his case, but another report had information that hurt his case. They got this information in a meeting with Jerry, who wanted to give it to them face to face.

With a folder in front of him, Jerry said: "This is a report of an investigation that the company began after you took legal action against them."

Paola knew from his tone of voice that it wasn't good.

"It says there were four witnesses to the accident, whom they located and took statements from. The witnesses all said the same thing. They were standing on the street, looking up at a man in a bucket, and he stood up on the rim of the bucket and danced for them. When they saw him fall, they ran away, afraid they would be blamed for the accident."

"They were kids?" Paola said.

"Yeah, they were kids, between the ages of nine and eleven."

"But his coworker said the bucket tipped over and dumped him out. He didn't mention what those kids said."

"His coworker was lying to protect Danny. But he retracted that statement. What he said in a more recent statement agreed with what the kids said."

"I understand why you did it," she told Danny. "I know how you like to entertain people. But why did you lie about it?"

"*I didn't lie about it,*" Danny told her with tears in his eyes. "I didn't remember doing it. I still don't remember. When I fell, I hit my head, and I lost my memory."

"Did you know what Joe meant when he said you did it to yourself?"

"No, I didn't. I swear I didn't. If I'd known, I wouldn't have sued the company."

"Then why did he say you knew what he meant?"

"He thought I knew, so he didn't come out with it, and he was surprised when I sued the company. He called me and told me I was crazy. When I didn't understand, he realized that I didn't remember what I did, and then he told me."

"Oh, my god," she said, feeling sick.

"If you lost your memory," Jerry said after a silence, "you weren't lying. You were saying what you believed was true. And that should help you with your wife, but it won't help you with the company. When you performed on the bucket for those kids, you still had all your faculties, so you were reckless, and the company has cause for firing you."

"Did they fire him?" Paola asked.

"They didn't tell me. They have to tell him."

They did tell him, in a certified letter. They fired him for cause, and they stopped paying him compensation. The only thing he walked away with was his pension.

SEVEN

PAOLA STILL HAD questions, but with Danny standing in the hallway, holding the certified letter from the company, she knew it wasn't a good time to ask them. She stood by him, feeling his pain not only from losing his job as a lineman but also from losing his identity as an employee of the company where he had worked for twenty-six years, and where his father had worked for more than forty years. She knew he had been waiting to tell his father about the lawsuit until after he won it, and now he would have to tell his father he had lost everything.

At one level she understood why he had performed for the children who were looking up at him. Danny had a need to entertain people, to make them love him. So she could easily imagine him dancing on the rim of the bucket to entertain those children. But at another level she didn't understand why he had that need. Did it come from his being the youngest of five children and the only boy?

With her arm around Danny's waist she led him gently into the kitchen, committed to helping him deal with his loss and start a new career with the family business. As an electrician, he wouldn't be working with the main power lines, but he would be working with the wires and the connections fed by those lines, so there would be some continuity.

On the kitchen counter she found a note from Briana, who had gone to a friend's house and would not be home for dinner. School was over, so there was no homework for her to do. She had a part-time job at the pharmacy on Palisade Avenue, but not much else to keep her busy.

Paola crumpled the note and asked: "Would you like a beer?"

"Yeah, sure," Danny said dully.

She got two bottles of Bud out of the refrigerator, opened them both, and handed one to Danny. Since the weather was nice, she suggested that they go outside, and he followed her out onto the deck, where they had chairs, a table, and a grill. The deck was shaded by a maple tree that they had planted a few weeks after Briana was born.

They sat for a while in silence, and then she said: "I want to leave this whole thing behind us, but before we move on, I have a few questions. Okay?"

"Okay."

"When did Joe call you?"

"About a week ago."

"What did he tell you?"

"He told me what really happened that day."

"Did you try to stop the lawsuit?"

"Yeah. I called Jerry, and I asked him to stop it, but it was too late. The company had already done their investigation."

"Did Joe know what was in their report?"

"No. He called me when he heard I was suing the company. He was worried that they'd find those kids and get their story."

"Did you know he changed his statement?"

"I didn't know until Jerry told us. But I don't blame him. It must have gotten him into trouble to cover up for me."

"So you haven't talked with Joe since he called you and told you what really happened?"

"No, I haven't," Danny said. "I need to call him and find out what they did to him."

"Before you call him," Paola said, "I need to tell you how much it hurts me that you knew a week ago what really happened and you didn't tell me."

Danny sighed. "I'm sorry. I was hoping that the company wouldn't find out what really happened."

"But that wasn't an acceptable reason for not telling me."

"I know it wasn't. I should have told you."

She took a swig of beer and said: "Well, now we can leave the whole thing behind us and move on."

He waited for her to continue.

"You need to start a new career."

"I know, but I have no idea what I could do."

"You could work for Borgatti Electric."

"You mean work for you?"

"You wouldn't work for me. You'd work for the business."

"But you own the business," he pointed out.

"Is that an obstacle?"

"I don't know. I guess it's not."

"But it would bother you."

"Maybe it would," he said after a moment. "I never imagined working for a business owned by my wife."

It didn't take her very long to find a solution. "Well, we could own the business together, fifty-fifty. Would that help?"

He nodded. "Yeah. That would help."

She extended her hand to him. "Partner?"

"Partner." He clasped her hand with enthusiasm.

She arranged to meet with her parents the next evening after dinner. She drove to their house and found them in the living room watching a news program. They were sitting in their usual chairs, and on the table between them was a pair of brandy glasses. From the coffee beans that floated in the clear liquid Paola could tell they were having sambuca, evidently anticipating a need to fortify themselves for a serious conversation.

Without waiting for the current segment of the program to end, her father turned off the television and asked: "Would you like a drink?"

"No, thanks," she said, sitting down on the sofa.

"You said you needed to talk with us about something," her mother said, prompting her.

"It's about Danny. He lost his job."

"What?" her father said. "What happened?"

"The company fired him."

"Why did they fire him?"

"He wouldn't do the job they wanted him to do." This was the version that she and Danny had agreed to give their parents.

Essentially it was true because if Danny had accepted the job of managing work crews the company never would have found out that he caused the accident. And their parents didn't need that information.

"Well, he should have done it," her mother said. "What's he going to do now?"

"He's going to work for our business."

"You mean as an electrician?" her father said.

"Yeah. He's licensed."

"He's licensed to do the kind of work he did for the electric company but not the kind of work we do, so he needs to get licensed for that."

"I'll ask Anthony what he needs to do."

"What about your healthcare benefits?" her mother asked, knowing that Paola and Briana had been covered by Danny's plan with the company.

"We'll get into a family plan."

"That'll be costly," her father said. "I mean with his condition."

"His shoulder's fine. He's almost done with the therapy."

Her father took a sip of sambuca. "So Danny's going to work for you?"

"He's going to work for the business," she said. "He's going to be my partner, so he should own half the business."

"Why should he own half the business?"

"So he can feel he's working for himself, not for me."

"I understand, but I want to keep the business in the family."

"It'll still be in the family. Danny's my husband."

"He's your husband now, but what if you get divorced?"

"We won't get divorced," Paola said definitely. "We've been married for nineteen years."

"I know a couple," her mother said, "who'd been married for twenty-five years, and they got divorced."

"All right. We can put in the agreement that if we get divorced, then his half of the business comes back to me."

"What if you die before he does?" her father asked. "Who will get your half?"

"Briana will. And if anything happens to both of us, Briana will get the whole thing."

"Yeah, that will keep it in the family."

"So are you okay with this?"

"I guess I am. But I want Anthony to write the agreement."

"Of course," she said. "I wouldn't use anyone else."

She knew it would be a lot harder telling his parents he had lost his job, but he couldn't put it off for long because his father was bound to hear it from someone, and it would be much better if his father heard it from him, so the next evening they drove to Woodlawn.

His father was in the living room watching the Yankees game, and his mother was in the kitchen cleaning up from dinner. Paola stayed with his father, watching the game, while Danny went into the kitchen and got his mother. They waited until Jeter had stretched a single into a double before starting the conversation.

"I lost my job," Danny told his parents.

"You lost your job?" his father said with a frown of disbelief.

"Yeah. The company fired me."

"How could the company fire you?" His father seemed to question their right to do such a thing to his son. "What was the reason?"

"I wouldn't do the job they wanted me to do."

"What was the job?"

"Managing work crews."

His father blinked as if he was having trouble with his eyes. "Are you telling me they offered you a job managing work crews, and you wouldn't do it?"

"That's right."

"Did you try it?"

"Yeah. I tried it for a while, and I didn't like it."

"What didn't you like about it?"

"I didn't like watching other people do things while I was doing nothing."

Paola was following the conversation closely, and so far Danny had avoided outright lying.

"You're out of your mind," his father said, shaking his head. "Do you realize how many guys would give their right arm to have that job?"

"I don't care. I didn't want it. I wanted my old job."

"You couldn't do your old job."

"Yeah, I could have."

His father took a long, deep breath. "The company's opinion was based on a doctor's report. What's your opinion based on?"

"It's based on how I feel."

"Well, how you feel doesn't matter."

Seeing that they were getting nowhere, Paola intervened, saying: "Tell them what you're going to do now."

"I'm going to work for Borgatti Electric," Danny told them positively.

"Your family's business?" his father asked her.

"*Our* business. We're going to be partners, fifty-fifty."

"You're letting him buy half the business?"

"I'm giving it to him."

"That's very generous of you," his mother said.

"We're husband and wife. We should share things equally."

"Well, maybe it's time you did something on your own," his father finally said. "At times I thought about doing something on my own, but I never got around to it."

"Then we have your blessing?"

"You have our blessing." His father looked at Paola, saying: "Your husband's a lucky guy."

"We're both lucky," Paola said. "We have each other."

Anthony drew up an agreement in which Paola transferred half the ownership of the business to Danny. Her father made sure the agreement provided for the business to stay in the family, and he said it was all right for Paola to sign.

After checking the requirements Anthony explained to Danny what he would have to do in order to be licensed as an electrician. It was basically what Paola had done, except that the required period of experience was shortened due to Danny's experience with the electric company. He had to take classes on wiring and installation, and he had to pass the licensing examination. In the meantime he could work as an apprentice, as Paola had done. He accepted the process, though he argued that the required period of experience should have been shortened even more because of his years as a lineman.

By the week after the middle of July he was working for the business, being mentored by Al, the most senior employee. Al was in his early sixties, and unlike some of the younger guys, he had a lot of patience as well as a sense of humor. Danny respected his experience, and Al enjoyed Danny's stories, so they got along fine.

The only problem occurred when Al took a week off for his daughter's wedding, and Paola assigned Danny to Nelson. They had a series of repair jobs, beginning with a job in downtown Yonkers and ending with a job in Tarrytown.

When they returned at the end of the day she asked Danny how things had gone, and he asked her to wait until they were in the car. To avoid using two cars, they went to the office together and they went home together, usually with Paola driving so that Danny could rest his shoulder and his arm. They were all right for the kind of jobs that he was doing, but after using them all day they sometimes bothered him, and turning the steering wheel of a car required a motion that made things worse.

"Can you do me a favor?" he asked as she pulled out onto Nepperhan Avenue.

"Sure. What?" She couldn't imagine what he wanted.

"Don't ever assign me to him again."

"You mean Nelson?"

"Whatever his name is."

"His name is Nelson."

"Where did he get a name like that?"

"From his parents, I assume."

"Well, it doesn't sound a like a spic name."

"Don't use that word."

"Spic? Why not?"

"It's hateful, that's why."

"I don't hate him. I just don't want to work with him."

"But he's one of our best employees. You could learn a lot from him."

"Yeah, I could learn how to use a knife."

"You know," she said after a painful silence, "I never heard you talk that way until you thought the company had given your job to a Puerto Rican. Did you always feel that way about Latinos?"

"I never had much to do with them. They didn't hang out at the places where I went."

"You must have gone to school with them."

"There were a few, but not many."

"Well, there are more now, so you better get used to them."

"Why do I have to get used to them?"

"Because we live in the same town, the same county, the same state—"

"Okay, okay. We live in the same country, but I don't have to work with them."

She could have reminded him that though he owned half the business, she still had control, and she could assign him to anyone she wanted, especially since he was only an apprentice and wasn't allowed to work on his own. Instead, she said: "I can schedule around your prejudice, but I don't like having this difference between us. I mean, it's not a difference in taste, it's a difference in values."

"It's not a big deal," he told her.

"It's a big enough deal so you don't want to work with him."

"All right, all right, I'll work with him."

They waited in silence for the light at Roberts Avenue, and when it was green she turned left and headed up the hill, asking: "Where did you get it from?"

"Where did I get what from?"

"Your prejudice against Latinos."

"Why did I have to get it from somewhere?"

"Because you weren't born with it."

"Well, I guess I got it from the neighborhood where I grew up."

"That figures. I bet you had a name for Italians."

"We called them guineas."

"I bet you never imagined that you'd marry a guinea."

"I never did. What's your point?"

"My point is, you never imagined working with a spic, but now you've got one as an employee in your business."

"I didn't hire him. You did."

"But it's your business as well as mine. And Nelson is a damn good employee."

"Okay, I get it," Danny said as if he had enough of this conversation.

In early August she was in the office, working on the job schedule for the next day, when Al came in and closed the door behind him, asking: "Can we talk?"

"Yeah. What's on your mind?"

Al sat down heavily in the chair next to her desk, looking uncomfortable. "It's about Danny. I think you should know what's happening with him."

She swallowed. "Tell me."

"Well, the first few weeks he was doing fine, and we were working well together. But the past few weeks he's been acting different."

"What do you mean?"

"I'll give you an example. We were on a job yesterday, and he had trouble understanding what he was supposed to do. He was confused about it."

"Did you explain it to him?"

"Yeah, I did. I explained it several times, and he still didn't understand. I could have been speaking in Japanese."

"Has that ever happened before?"

"It's been happening over the past few weeks."

She hadn't observed that behavior at home, but with her attention divided between him and Briana, she could have missed it.

Al continued. "And when he understands the job, he has

trouble doing it. I mean, he has trouble with his hands."

"What kind of trouble?"

"The kind you have when your hands are cold."

"But that could be from his injury."

"It could be. But he has trouble with *both* hands. When he tries to connect two wires, he can't make his hands work together."

She hadn't observed that either.

"I didn't understand what was happening," Al said, "until I noticed that after he goes into a bathroom, within about ten minutes he acts like he's high."

"You think he's taking drugs?"

"I hate to say it because he's your husband, but that's what I think. I've seen it before with my nephew who lives in the city."

"Oh, my god," she said, wondering if Danny was taking the drug he had used to kill the pain from his surgeries. She had noticed that over the past few weeks he had been withdrawing more than the usual amounts of money from the cash machine, and when she questioned him about it he explained that he was paying cash for things instead of using his credit card. Believing him, she hadn't questioned him further, but now she realized that he could have been using the money to buy that drug because the doctor had stopped prescribing it.

"I'm sorry," Al said. "But I thought you should know."

"You were right to tell me. I'll take him off the schedule until we can figure this out."

"You don't have to take him off the schedule. I'll work with him. I'll just have to keep an eye on him."

She waited until after dinner, when they were sitting out on the deck, to raise the issue. She had decided not to reveal what Al had told her because it would affect the relationship between the two men. Instead, she simply asked: "Are you taking drugs?"

"Why are you asking?" he said defensively.

"I'm asking because I want to know."

He was silent for a while, and then he said: "I'm not taking drugs on a regular basis, but every so often I take a painkiller."

"You still have a lot of pain in your shoulder?"

"Every so often."

"How often?"

"Oh, I don't know. Maybe once or twice a week."

"So maybe once or twice a week you take a painkiller?"

"Yeah, that's right."

"Where do you get them?"

"I buy them from a doctor. Not the one who did the surgery. I asked that doctor for more, but he wouldn't give me another prescription."

"So you buy them in the black market."

"It's not a black market, it's a gray market."

"It's still against the law."

"Well, what am I supposed to do? When I have pain, I need something for it."

"I understand. But you can get addicted to those drugs, and they have terrible side effects."

"I don't care about the side effects. I can live with them."

"Maybe you can live with them, but they can affect your ability to do your job."

"They haven't so far," he said with a look that defied her to challenge him.

"They will eventually. You need to see a doctor and at least find out if you *are* addicted."

"What if I am?"

"They can treat you for it."

Without further argument he got up and went inside and returned with his laptop, which he handed to her, saying: "Here. You can find a doctor."

She didn't know what to search for, and she tried some different key words before she found doctors who treated addiction to opioids. There were more than she expected, and there were even several who had nearby offices.

He pulled his chair over so that he could see them on the screen.

"This one looks good," she said, displaying the credentials of a doctor who specialized in pain medicine and rehabilitation. "His office is right across from St. John's."

"He's a wog," Danny said.

"You mean an Indian?"

"Whatever he is, I don't want to see him."

She displayed the next one. "What about him?"

"Are you kidding? He wears a turban."

The next doctor was Chinese.

"A chink? No way."

The next was a woman.

"No way."

He finally agreed to see a white male doctor whose office was on Yonkers Avenue.

They drove there a few days later, and after waiting almost an hour Danny was led away from the reception area by a young woman. Paola didn't go with him because she was ready to support him but not to buffer him.

Much later the young woman invited her to join Danny in the doctor's office.

"Mrs. O'Dwyer," the doctor said, extending his hand. "I'm Dr. Moore."

"It's nice to meet you," Paola said, shaking his hand.

"Please sit down."

She sat down next to Danny in front of a desk.

"I want you to hear directly from me what I say about Danny. And based on my assessment of him, I believe he's addicted to opioids."

She looked at Danny, who sat there impassive, and she took the hand that was dangling below the seat of his chair. He was sitting to her left, so it was the hand on his bad side, and it felt like it was reflecting pain from his shoulder.

"We have to do a series of blood tests," the doctor said, "and then we can develop a program for treatment."

"What's the treatment?" Paola asked.

"It's a combination of therapy, detoxification, and recovery support. I'll give you a writeup that describes and explains the process. Mrs. O'Dwyer, you'll play a key role in it. Your husband will need your full support."

"He has my full support."

"Good. Then we can talk about finding him a therapist. I'll give you a list of people we use. They're in this area."

"Will he be able to keep working?"

"He's going to have withdrawal effects, which will get worse before they get better."

"What are those effects?"

"Anxiety, depression, muscle aches, body pains, tiredness, trouble sleeping—"

"If he's tired, why would he have trouble sleeping?"

"It's not the normal kind of tiredness. He also might have chills, nausea, vomiting, diarrhea, and other effects. The writeup includes the typical effects."

"So during that time he shouldn't be working?"

"No, he shouldn't. He'll need time off."

"How long will he need?"

"It could take several months. But after a month, the worst should be over."

"What happens then?"

Dr. Moore blinked as if he didn't understand. "If you're asking what happens at the end of the program, you take measures to prevent him from getting addicted again."

"What kind of measures?"

"They're in the writeup, but the most important thing is to avoid taking painkillers."

"What if I have pain?" Danny asked.

"From what you told me, pain wasn't your only reason for taking that drug. You had other reasons. So if you have pain, you can take ibuprofen. But even that you'll have to control. You can't eat it like popcorn."

When they left the doctor's office with the writeup of the treatment program and the list of therapists, Paola felt better, though she wondered about Danny's other reasons for taking that drug. Was he doing it to get high? Was he doing it to escape from reality? Was he doing it to help him deal with his present situation?

That night, while they were lying in bed, she asked him about it. "The doctor said you had other reasons for taking that drug. I mean, other than for pain."

"He doesn't know," Danny said. "He's only guessing."

"But *were* there other reasons?"

After a long silence he said: "There might have been. I know this sounds crazy, but I miss being up in the bucket, and taking the drug made me feel like I was back up there."

"You miss being up in the bucket?"

"Yeah. I miss being up there above people."

She thought she understood. "And now you're here below with people."

"It's a big change, and the drug might have been helping me to get used to it."

"Well, you don't need a drug to get used to it."

"I know I don't. And don't worry, I'll follow the program."

The next morning, taking the day off from work, Paola studied the writeup of the program. She also went to the internet and read about opioid addiction. She was surprised to learn that it had become an epidemic, with more people dying from opioid abuse than from automobile accidents. Knowing there were millions of people in her situation who loved and cared for an opioid addict, she had less trouble accepting it.

Later that morning, sitting in the kitchen, they addressed the question of whether they should tell their daughter and their parents about it. They decided without much discussion not to tell their parents, who didn't need to know. But it took them a while to decide not to tell Briana. They agreed that eventually they would tell her, but that now when Briana was about to start her sophomore year in high school, they shouldn't lay such a burden on her.

From the list of therapists Danny selected one who had an office on North Broadway, and he made an appointment for the next day. He liked the guy, who had grown up in the Bronx, and he started meeting with him twice a week.

In the meantime the doctor took him off the drug in steps, and when he stopped taking it he began to have withdrawal effects, which included muscle pain, body aches, and trouble sleeping. Lying next to a man who was writhing in agony, Paola also had trouble sleeping, and there were days when they both walked around like zombies.

As the doctor predicted, the withdrawal effects got worse over the next few days, and they peaked one night when Danny ended up kneeling on the bathroom floor with his head bowed over the toilet, shaking and retching.

Alarmed by the sounds, Briana rushed into the bathroom, asking: "What's wrong with Dad?"

"He's sick," Paola said. "But don't worry, he'll be all right."

"Shouldn't we take him to the hospital?"

"He's seen a doctor, and he's being treated."

"What's he being treated for?"

"Food poisoning." For now this was close enough to the truth.

As the weeks passed the effects faded, and the doctor said that Danny could go back to work. Paola assigned him to Al, who she knew would take good care of him.

That Friday, needing to talk with someone outside of her family, she met Gabby at O'Malley's, and she told her friend about Danny's addiction and his treatment.

After listening with sympathy Gabby asked: "Is he completely off the drugs?"

"Yeah. They gave him an opioid-replacement drug for a while," Paola said, "but then they took him off that. So now he's completely off the drugs."

"If he's completely off the drugs, you did well."

"I didn't do it. Danny did it."

"But you helped him."

"Maybe I did. But I could have helped him more if I'd seen it coming and if I'd stopped him from getting addicted."

"You didn't know what could have happened. Most people don't know, and that's why we have thousands of people addicted to opioids. So you should blame the system, beginning with the drug companies that design those drugs so people will get addicted to them."

"They don't do that deliberately."

"Yeah, they do. If people get addicted, the drug companies make more money."

"I don't want to believe that."

"You better believe it," Gabby said. "They're like the food and beverage companies that design products so people will get addicted to them."

"Okay, okay. I blame the system. But we're not mindless victims of it. We have to accept some responsibility."

"Yeah, we do. Not everyone who takes opioids as painkillers gets addicted to them."

Paola reflected. "You know, the doctor who treated Danny's addiction said that pain wasn't his only reason for taking that drug."

"Yeah, there are addicts who didn't start taking opioids as painkillers. They started taking them to get a high."

"Well, that's what I think is the other reason. Danny said he got a high from being up in the bucket. He said he missed being up in the bucket, and taking the drug made him feel like he was back up there."

"I hope he realizes that the drug didn't actually put him back up there. It only made him *feel* like he was back up there."

"I think he realizes that the drug didn't help him," Paola said. "At least he knows how much it hurt him to get off it."

"A lot of addicts don't ever get off it."

"They don't? Ever?"

"No, not ever," Gabby said as if she knew of such cases. "Even if they get treatment, they still might have to go through life on opioid-replacement drugs."

"Is that because they have a physiological need for the drugs?"

"They might have a physiological need, but they might also have a psychological need."

"You mean they need whatever the drugs do for them."

"Yeah. But if Danny got off the drugs, then he must have also overcome the psychological need for them."

"I believe he did," Paola said as a matter of faith. "If I didn't believe it, I'd worry about him, and that wouldn't help him."

"No, it wouldn't. So he has your full support."

"Yeah. He'll always have it."

After taking a sip of wine Gabby asked: "What about Briana?"

"She doesn't know about his addiction. We didn't want to lay that on her."

"How did you explain what was happening with Danny?"

"She didn't see what was happening with him, except one time when he was in the bathroom, retching his guts out. I told her it was food poisoning."

"But you'll tell her eventually?"

"Yeah, we will. We'll tell her when she needs to know about it. But for the time being she doesn't need to know about it."

"I assume your parents don't know about it."

"Lord, no. They wouldn't understand."

Gabby smiled. "You sound like you *do* understand."

"I don't understand," Paola said, "but I won't make a judgment like my parents would. If you love someone, you accept him no matter what he does."

"But there's a limit."

"Maybe there is, but I'm nowhere near it."

"That's good. He's a lucky guy."

"We're both lucky," Paola said, realizing that she had said the same thing to Danny's father. And she still meant it.

On Saturday they celebrated Danny's first week back at work by having dinner with her parents at D & V. Briana would have joined them, but that night she was babysitting.

To explain Danny's absence from work, Paola had told her parents that he needed time off for more therapy on his shoulder, which was at least indirectly true, and now she was happy to report to them that he was back at work and doing well.

"Yeah, Al told me," her father said.

"Al's the best," Danny said appreciatively.

"You like working as an electrician?" her father asked him after a silence.

"Yeah, I like it."

"It's not like working on the high wires, but it's satisfying. You install things for people, you fix things for people, and you feel good at the end of the day."

"Yeah, you do. When you're up in the air you only see birds and squirrels. Down on the ground you see people."

"Sometimes people are difficult," Paola admitted. "But usually they're fine."

"The toughest ones," her father said, "are the guys who did the wiring themselves and won't admit it. They always blame the previous electrician."

"From what I've seen," Danny said, "we do a lot of fixing things that weren't done right to begin with."

"Well, don't complain. That gives us business."

With the waitress prompting them to order, they stopped talking to peruse the menus.

After they had ordered, her father asked: "Did the therapy help your shoulder?"

"Oh, yeah. I have almost full motion."

"That's more than I have. My arthritis is getting worse. So maybe I should try that therapy."

Paola said: "You should go to the therapist who helped Danny. You'd like her."

"The therapist is a girl?"

"Yeah. She has a doctorate in physical therapy."

"She's also pretty," Danny said. "And even though she couldn't weigh more than a hundred pounds, she's very strong."

"Briana's strong," Paola said. "I think she could be a good physical therapist."

"Does she still want to be a nurse?" her mother asked.

"Yeah. She was very good with Danny."

"Now, where's she tonight?" her father asked.

"She's babysitting for Gabriella."

"How is Gabriella?"

"She's doing well. She's a school psychologist in Yonkers."

"Really? Is that a good job?"

"It's the job she always wanted. And her husband's a teacher, so together they have a good income."

"Well, with Danny back, we're at full strength, and we should have a good year. Are we going to get that job with Caputo?"

"I think we will," Paola said, having placed a competitive bid for the job. "The guy's a real hard ass, but he knows we'll do a good job."

"So let's drink to you and Danny," her father said, raising his glass of red wine.

As they raised their glasses Paola said a silent prayer.

EIGHT

Now that Briana was a junior in high school she had more
homework, and they didn't want her to do it lying on her bed, as
she was inclined to do, so they converted the spare bedroom into
a workspace for her, with a proper desk and bookshelves and file
cabinets. She liked having her own workspace in addition to her
bedroom.

Danny, who had hated the computer on which he had to do
workshops for the electric company, had found other uses for it,
so they moved it to the basement, which the previous owners of
the house had finished and made into a party room complete with
a bar, stools, a sofa, chairs, a refrigerator, and a stereo cabinet.
Now after dinner, while Briana did her homework and Paola
watched television, Danny went down to the basement and played
on his computer.

A few weeks after school started Paola met with the developer
of a residential building to convince him that Borgatti Electric
could do the job that they had bid on. His name was Vito Caputo,
and years ago when he was still doing small jobs as a general
contractor he had used her father's services. Her father had a good
relationship with him, but he decided that if Paola was going to
run the business, she should learn to negotiate with developers on
her own, so she went to the meeting without him, taking Danny
with her as co-owner of the business.

Vito had his company headquarters in one of the office towers
he had built in White Plains. It was on the top floor, which gave
him a view of his real estate empire. He was a handsome man who
must have been her father's age but looked younger.

He received her and Danny graciously, asking them if they
would like coffee and inviting them to sit down at a conference
table.

"How's your father?" he asked Paola.

"He's fine. He still works a few days a week, but I'm running the business now."

"Your father must trust you."

"He trusts me completely. He taught me everything I know about the business."

"I usually don't get involved in these details. I leave them to my general contractor. But this is a big job, and I want to make sure you have the resources to handle it."

"We have the resources. We're hiring extra men for it."

"Have they worked with you before?"

"Yeah. They've all worked with us before."

"And they're all licensed?"

"They're all licensed."

"You understand that the city looks at us closely."

"I understand." She knew that Vito was a controversial figure in his hometown and that everything he did was scrutinized.

"The other thing is, we have a tight deadline, so you'd have to stay on schedule."

"I know. We're used to tight deadlines."

Vito looked at her as if he still couldn't believe he was dealing with a woman. "Based on my experience with your father, I'm inclined to approve you for the job, but it would help if you could lower your bid a little."

"By how much?"

"Ten percent."

She pushed back her chair and started to rise.

"What are you doing?"

"I'm leaving," she said. "If you don't want to pay for quality work, then we don't want to do the job."

Vito grinned at her. "Sit down. I was only testing you."

"I don't need testing," she told him firmly. "I know what I'm doing."

"I believe you do. Well, you have the job. And give my regards to your father."

When they were going down in the elevator Danny said: "You really stood up to that guy."

"You have to stand up to guys like him. If you don't, they take advantage of you."

"How did you learn that?"

"I learned it from my father."

"Well, he should be proud of you."

"I don't know. I guess he should be."

Danny put an arm around her, reassuring her.

Two weeks later they began work on the job. They had two teams of electricians, with Al as leader of one team and Nelson as leader of the other team. She assigned Danny to work with Al, avoiding the problem he had with Nelson, but after a few days it became apparent that Nelson's team was falling behind schedule.

"What's the problem?" she asked Nelson at the end of the third day.

"Oh, it's that temp guy."

"Which temp guy?"

"The older one."

"What's the matter with him?"

"I think he feels he shouldn't be working for me."

"Because he's older?"

"No, because he's white."

She realized that within the deadline she wouldn't have time to rid the guy of his prejudice nor time to replace him, so she asked Nelson: "What if I switch him with Danny?"

"You think it would work any better?"

"I don't know, but at least Danny has a stake in the job."

"Okay. Let's try it."

That night at home she talked with Danny about the switch. They were at the dinner table after Briana had excused herself to do her homework when Paola raised the issue, saying: "We're falling behind schedule on this job."

"How could that be? Our team's on track."

"I know it is, but the other team isn't."

"Oh, is Nelson having a problem?" he asked as if he would have expected it.

"Yeah. It's one of his temp guys."

"What's the problem?"

"The guy feels he shouldn't be working for Nelson."

"He does? Well, I can understand why."

"Danny," she said with urgency, "if we don't complete this job on schedule, we won't get any more business from Vito."

"Then maybe you should replace the temp guy."

"I don't have time to replace him. The only thing I can do at this point is switch him with a member of your team."

"Well, don't look at *me*," Danny said. "I don't want to work for Nelson."

"I don't want to do a lot of things," she said, "but I do them because I have to."

"Are you telling me I have to switch with that guy?"

"I'm asking you to switch with him."

Danny was silent for a long time, and then he finally said: "If I did it, would it help you?"

"It would help *us*. If we do a good job for Vito, he'll not only give us more business, he'll tell other people we did a good job."

"Okay. I'll do it."

They made the switch the next day, and Nelson's team got back on schedule.

As she watched Danny working with Nelson she felt as if she had helped him make a breakthrough. By the end of the job, which they completed within the deadline, Danny was acting like Nelson was his buddy. In fact, on the last day he invited Nelson to join them for a celebration at O'Malley's.

For the next several weeks things were going well. Briana was getting good grades, Danny was doing a good job, and Paola was seeing a growth in the business. Then one evening, after they came home from work and she was in the kitchen going through the mail, she noticed an unfamiliar item on their credit card statement. The amount was more than two hundred dollars, so it stood out among the regular charges for groceries and household items.

As usual Danny had gone to take a shower and change into

clean clothes, but as soon as he appeared in the kitchen Paola asked him about the item.

"Oh, that's for software," he said, casually opening the door of the refrigerator.

"Software? What kind of software?"

He took a bottle of beer out of the refrigerator and faced her sheepishly. "Video games."

"You're playing video games on your computer?"

"Well, I'm not *working* on my computer. I work all day."

"I know, but games?" She didn't understand. "What kind of games?"

"They're usually quests or contests or battles."

"What are they good for?"

"They're good for the mind. They're also good for hand and eye coordination."

"Okay. But I hope you won't spend this much every month on video games."

"I won't. I mean, there could be smaller amounts." He finally opened the beer and took a swig. "But what's the big deal? You spend money on personal things."

"I don't spend that much on my hair."

"Well, those things add up."

She couldn't believe they were having this conversation, and she didn't like what it was doing to them, so she ended it by saying: "All right. You have a point. And I wasn't complaining about the charge, I was only asking about it."

"I should have told you about it," he said, meeting her halfway.

It could have been her imagination, but it seemed like he was spending more and more time playing on his computer, and there were nights when he came upstairs after she had gone to bed. But she didn't worry about it until Briana started going down to the basement, presumably after finishing her homework. By the time Briana came up to her room it was well past her bedtime, and she had more trouble than usual getting up in the morning.

To see what they were up to, Paola went down to the basement one evening and found them sitting side by side, playing a game on the computer. It was some kind of battle game, and the object was to kill as many people as possible on the enemy side using weapons that fired laser beams. A direct hit would blow the enemy to pieces.

After watching them for a while Paola said: "I don't see the point of this game."

"The point is to defeat the enemy," Briana said.

"But it's so violent. You really like blowing people to pieces?"

"Yeah, I really do. It's a harmless outlet for my feelings of aggression."

"I didn't know you had feelings of aggression."

"We all have feelings of aggression. Even you do, mom," Briana added, "though you'd never admit it."

"I admit it. I feel like smashing that computer."

"So why don't you come and play with us?"

"I have better things to do," Paola said. "I want you in bed by ten. *Capeesh?*"

"Aw, that's too early. How about eleven?"

"It's not negotiable. And I hope you finished your homework before you came down here."

"I did. Don't worry."

Paola was still awake that night when Danny finally came to bed. It probably wasn't a good time to talk about it, but she couldn't wait.

"I don't want Briana to play those games with you."

"You don't? Why not?"

"Because they're violent. They teach her that it's all right to kill. In fact, they teach her that killing is fun."

"They're just games. She knows we're not killing real people."

"Maybe she does. But there must be times when she doesn't know the difference."

"You're using your imagination too much."

"Well, that's another problem I have with those games. They don't leave anything to the imagination."

He was silent for a while, and then he said: "You should be

glad I'm doing something with my daughter. Most fathers don't do anything with their daughters."

"Where did you get that idea?"

"From listening to the guys at work. They only do things with their sons."

"Do they play video games with their sons?"

"At times, yeah. But more often they play sports with them."

"So why don't you play a sport with your daughter?"

"I can't play sports anymore," he said. "I'm on the disabled list. Remember?"

"Yeah," Paola said, touched. "You could still coach her. Or you could play another kind of game with her. There must be video games that are educational."

"There probably are. But would they be fun?"

"I don't know. You could look for one. And in the meantime I don't want her to play those violent games with you."

"How do I stop her?"

"You tell her she can't play with you. And I'll tell her she can't play those games with you."

"Okay," he said, rolling over without a goodnight kiss.

The next day she got home from work in time to meet with Briana in the kitchen after school. Briana was at the table having cookies and milk while listening to music through the wires that ran from her phone to her ears. It dismayed Paola that her daughter couldn't do anything without being connected with her phone.

"Could you unplug for a minute?" she said, sitting down at the table to have a conversation.

Briana delayed but finally, reluctantly removed the earbuds, saying: "Yeah. What?"

"Your father and I talked last night, and we agreed that you shouldn't play those violent games with him."

"I bet that was your idea."

"It was, but your father agreed. He understands that it's not a good use of your time."

"So what would be a better use of my time?"

"Reading, or even watching television."

"They have violence on television."

"I know, but you wouldn't participate in that violence."

"I'd still watch it. What's the difference?"

Paula took a deep breath before saying: "It's the difference between being a spectator and being a perpetrator. But I still don't want you to watch violence on television."

"What *do* you want me to watch on television?"

"Programs about nature and science. You always liked them."

"I did when I was younger, but I don't like them anymore."

"Well, your father's going to look for a video game that's not violent, and when he finds one you can play that with him. But you're not allowed to play violent games with him."

Briana said nothing, she only gave her mother a resentful look before reconnecting the earbuds and shutting her out.

On Friday she met Gabby at O'Malley's. It had been a few weeks since they last got together, so they had a lot to catch up on.

"I see that Danny's not here tonight," Gabby said after looking at the round table where he usually entertained his audience of guys. "Is he at Brennan's?"

"No, he took Briana to the movies."

"What movie are they seeing?"

"I can't remember the name of it. I only know it's some kind of science fiction."

"The kids like science fiction. It enables them to escape from reality."

"Is reality so bad for them?"

"I think it is. I mean, it's worse for them than it was for us. We only had the Gulf War, but they have terrorists."

"If they're worried about terrorists, why would they want to see movies about them?"

"Movies make the terrorists unreal. If someone gets his head chopped off in the movies, it's only in the movies."

"I guess it is. But I'd rather see a movie about real life."

"When we were their age, did we see movies about real life?"

"I think we did. From what I remember, they were mostly about teenage love."

"You mean teenage sex."

"But those movies weren't explicit. The sex was always in the background."

"Yeah, but it was always in our heads."

"I guess it was."

"The kids at school think about sex all the time. I tell them that when they get to be my age, they'll think about sex only ninety percent of the time."

Paola laughed. "I wish I could say that, but now I think about something else most of the time."

"What do you think about?"

"Danny. He spends the evenings playing video games."

"What kind of games?"

"Violent games. The object is to kill as many people as possible on the enemy side."

"Those games are very popular."

"I don't know why."

"They provide an outlet for feelings of aggression."

"That's what Briana said."

"Does she play them?"

"She did play them. She was playing them with Danny, and I caught her. I told her she couldn't play that kind of game."

"And she stopped playing them?"

"At least she stopped playing them with her father."

"But he still plays them."

"Yeah, he does." After taking a sip of wine Paola asked: "Is it possible to get addicted to video games?"

"If you define addiction as compulsive use of video games that impairs a person's ability to fulfill other responsibilities, yeah, it's possible."

"Well, I don't think it's gone that far. I mean, he's fulfilling his responsibilities."

"How much time does he spend playing video games?"

"A lot. He goes down to the basement right after dinner, and he doesn't come upstairs until after I've gone to bed."

"Do you know what time he goes to bed?"

"I have no idea. I'm asleep by then. But one night I waited up for him, and it was after one in the morning when he finally came to bed."

"So how many hours a night is he playing?"

"I don't know. From four to six hours."

"How many nights a week?"

"Mm. We go out to dinner once a week, and we have dinner with my parents once a week, so let's say five nights a week."

"That's twenty to thirty hours a week," Gabby calculated. "If he's playing that much, it must impair his ability to fulfill his responsibilities to you."

Ignoring this observation, Paola said: "I just don't understand the attraction. What does he get from playing those stupid games?"

"He gets rewards. Those games are designed to reward the players, to give them satisfaction they can't get in the real world."

"You mean I've failed to give him satisfaction?"

Gabby shook her head. "You haven't failed to give him anything. He misses what he got from his job as a lineman. He misses the excitement, the feeling of being on top of the world."

"Yeah, he *loved* that job. He likes the job he has now, but he doesn't love it."

"Well, he has to accept that he can't ever have that job again, so he has to find other sources of satisfaction. I mean, other than addictions."

"So you think he's addicted to video games?"

"If he isn't," Gabby said, "he's becoming addicted. Twenty to thirty hours a week?"

Paola could feel her heart sinking. "What can I do?"

"You can encourage him to get treatment."

"Are there therapists who treat video game addiction?"

"I don't know, but I think he should see the therapist who helped him overcome his opioid addiction."

"That makes sense," Paola said. "He already has a relationship with that guy."

"Well, if he could overcome opioid addiction," Gabby said, touching her shoulder, "then he can overcome this addiction. And you can help him."

"I hope I can. I still love him as much as ever."

The next evening, after Briana had left the dinner table to finish her homework, Paola broached the subject with Danny, saying: "I'm worried about the video games."

"You don't have to worry," Danny said. "I've found games for Briana to play. They're not violent. They're educational."

"I'm not worried about her. I'm worried about you."

"Me?" He made a gesture with both hands pointing to himself. "Why me?"

"Because you spend twenty to thirty hours a week playing video games. I don't want you to get addicted to them."

"I won't get addicted to them. They're not like opioids."

"But you spend so much time playing them."

"I like playing them. I have fun playing them."

"There are other ways of having fun."

"I know, but wouldn't you rather have me at home where you know what I'm doing?"

"If I know you're playing video games, I'd rather have you out with your friends. At least you wouldn't be killing them."

He frowned in concentration before saying: "It's the violence you don't like."

"Yeah, it's the violence."

"What if I didn't play violent games?"

"That would be better. But if you spent as much time playing other games, it wouldn't be that much better. I mean, it could still become an addiction."

"You think because I got addicted to opioids I have a tendency to get addicted to things?"

"I don't know. I'm just worried that you could get addicted to video games."

He looked at her sadly, and then he said: "What do you want me to do about it?"

"I want you to go and see that therapist and tell him what you're doing. If he doesn't see a problem with it, then I won't either. Though," she added, "whatever he says, I'd like to see you doing other things."

"Okay, I'll see the therapist, and you think of other things you'd like to see me doing."

"Fair enough," she said, already beginning to think of them.

After one meeting with the therapist Danny admitted that he had gotten addicted to video games, and he promised that when he was done with the treatment he would never get addicted to anything again. In the meantime Paola had thought of other things she would like to see him doing. In fact, she had made a schedule of evening activities for a typical week. She assured Danny that it wasn't rigid, it was only a guideline.

On Sunday they would continue having dinner with her parents. On Monday they would rent a movie from Netflix, which Briana would select. On Tuesday they would play a board game at the dining room table. On Wednesday Danny and Briana would play nonviolent video games together, which could include card games. On Thursday they would watch television. On Friday Danny would go to O'Malley's and join his friends at the round table, and Paola would either have drinks with Gabby or stay at home while Briana had a friend for a sleepover. And on Saturday they would have dinner at D & V.

At first neither Danny nor Briana were happy with this schedule, but in time they got used to it and even made the most of it. The structure helped to bind them together as a family, and it provided for special occasions such as holidays, birthdays, and anniversaries.

NINE

THE REST OF that year went well, and at Thanksgiving, sitting at the table with her parents, her husband, her daughter, her brothers, her aunt, and her uncle, Paola felt she had a lot to be thankful for. Her parents were in good health, and Danny was being a good husband, a good father, and a good worker, and Briana was doing well in school, and the business was doing better than ever.

The new year began well, and they decided that they could afford to take Briana to a beach somewhere for the spring break. After looking online at the possibilities she found a package for a week at Punta Cana in the Dominican Republic. She asked Nelson about it, and he said it would be fine as long as the price was right. It was, so she booked the deal and announced to Danny and Briana that they were going to Punta Cana.

Their week in Punta Cana brought their family together as no experience had since the accident. They ate three meals together, they went to the beach together, and they did activities together, going on a zip-line and driving around on dune-buggies and exploring an underwater world in diving suits. When people said they had the best time on their vacation Paola wondered if they were being completely truthful, but when people asked her about their trip to Punta Cana she could say with her whole heart that they had the best time.

During that summer Briana worked at a day-care center. She loved this job so much that it made her want to be a pediatric nurse. It also kept her busy, so she wasn't lying around doing nothing as she had during the previous summer.

Continuing the family spirit of their spring break, Paola got tickets to several Yankees games, which they took the train to,

125

leaving from the Hastings station because she felt it was a safer place late at night than the Yonkers station. Danny at first rejected the idea of taking the train, insisting that he could handle the traffic, but then he realized the advantages of the train, which included having more than one beer at the game and avoiding long delays on the Major Deegan with passengers who urgently had to pee.

During that summer, as a result of recommendations from Vito Caputo, the business was awarded three big jobs. Since two of them were going at the same time, she had to divide her forces, putting Al in charge of one job and Nelson in charge of the other. She would have liked to put Danny in charge of a job, but he was still in the process of getting his license.

Everything changed in the middle of August when she received an invoice from a bank that, as far as she knew, they had never done business with. The amount due at the end of the month, as the first instalment of a business loan, was $10,399.60.

Believing it was a mistake, she called the bank and got a person who after being unhelpful for several minutes advised her to come and see the manager. Danny was out on a job at the time, so she left the office and got into her car and drove up Roberts Avenue to the commercial area where the bank was located. She remembered the bank from a warning her father had given her never to use it for anything because of his bad experiences, which included its making a loan to his father after he was dead.

The bank was on Roberts, around the corner from Palisade Avenue, right by the parking area, which luckily had an empty place. She went into the bank, asked for the manager, and after waiting about fifteen minutes she was admitted to his office.

The manager, who had cold blue eyes and a double chin, was installed behind a desk as if he had sat there all day without moving.

"Who are you?" he asked her

"I'm Paola O'Dwyer," she told him, handing her business card to him.

Looking at the card, the manager said: "Borgatti Electric?"

"Yeah, that's my family's business."

"Why are you here?"

"I got this invoice today," she said. She took it out of her pocketbook and handed it to him. "It must be a mistake."

The manager glanced at the invoice and said: "It's not a mistake."

"It must be. We've never done business with your bank."

"Yeah, you have. You have a loan from us."

Remembering how this bank had made a loan to her dead grandfather, Paola let her anger rise. "I'm sorry, but we don't have a loan from you."

The manager pressed a button on an intercom and said: "Deb, will you bring me the file on Borgatti Electric?"

Paola waited, feeling as if she was in a doctor's office waiting for the results of a mammogram.

It took a long time, but a woman with heavy perfume brought a file and handed it to the manager, who opened it and said: "Borgatti Electric. We made a loan to your company on August 6 for three hundred thousand dollars."

"Let me see that," Paola said, unable to imagine what might have happened.

The manager handed the file to her without a comment.

She thumbed through the document to the last page, and there was Danny's signature. She said: "I need a copy of this."

The manager summoned Deb, who returned and took the file away briskly.

"I have to talk with my lawyer," Paola said.

"You can talk with him all you want," the manager said, "but you do have a loan from us, and the first instalment is due by the end of this month."

"The loan has monthly instalments?"

The manager nodded. "That's how we structure all our loans."

"For how many years?"

"Three years."

With monthly instalments of more than ten thousand dollars, she didn't see how they could service the loan unless she and

Danny weren't paid salaries, and then what would they live on? She clung to the hope that for some reason the loan wasn't valid.

Ten minutes later she left with the document and returned to her office, where she closed the door and sat at her desk. Since they had never borrowed money before, she didn't know what a loan document should look like, so she read through it from beginning to end, marking places where she had questions.

She was still at her desk when Danny with his team returned from their job and came into the office. She wanted to wait until everyone else had left the office, so she made herself ask: "How did things go today?"

"Everything went well," he said, settling into the chair in front of her desk. "Nelson said that at the rate we're going, we should finish the job a day early."

"That would be great. You could move on to the next job."

"Are you all right?" he asked as if he had noticed something in her face.

"Yeah, I'm all right," she sighed.

"I'm glad. I was afraid that something had happened."

When they were finally alone in the office she said: "We got an invoice from a bank today."

"Oh, shit," he said, closing his eyes as if he was in pain. "They said they'd wait until I had a chance to repay them."

"A chance to repay the whole loan?"

"Yeah, they said they'd wait until October."

"But where would you have gotten the money?"

"The same way I lost it."

"Let's go back to the beginning," she said as calmly as possible, beginning to suspect how he had lost it. "Why did you get this loan from the bank?"

"I needed it to pay a debt."

"What kind of debt?"

"A gambling debt."

"Where were you gambling?"

"On the computer. Briana and I were playing card games on the computer. You know, like hearts and gin rummy. But then we discovered poker."

"I hope you didn't play poker with her."

"I only showed her what poker was. I played it after she went up to bed."

Paola sighed. "So you got addicted to gambling?"

"I wasn't addicted. I was only having fun. And for a while I was winning."

"You should have stopped playing while you were ahead."

"I know I should have," Danny said regretfully, "but I kept playing, and then I started losing."

"Why didn't you stop then?"

"I kept thinking I could make up my losses. By then I *was* addicted, and I didn't want to admit to you that I'd become an addict again."

"If you'd told me earlier, you wouldn't have ended up with so much debt."

"I know, I know." He bowed his head as if he was submitting to an execution.

It made her feel sorry for him. But she had to control her feelings and get to the bottom of the situation. "Who did you owe the money to?"

"The organization that runs the games."

"You mean the mob?"

"Yeah, the mob. I had no idea who they were until they tried to collect from me."

"Oh, my god. Did they threaten to break your knees?"

"No. They threatened to hurt Briana, so I had no choice."

She took a deep breath. "Now, let me get this straight. You ran up a debt to the mob by gambling online. You didn't realize how much it was, and when they tried to collect from you they threatened to hurt Briana."

"Yeah. So I needed a loan to pay them."

"Did you pay them everything you owed them?"

"I paid them what I owed them at the time. But I did some more gambling. I was hoping I could win enough to pay the bank by October."

"But you didn't win enough."

"No, I kept losing."

"So you still owe money to the mob?"

"Yeah, but not as much as I owed them before."

"Well, how much do you owe them now?"

"About fifty thousand dollars."

"Oh, Danny," she cried, losing control. "How could you have done this?"

He gazed at her sadly as if he had no idea how he could have done this, and it made her feel she should have known about it and stopped it.

That night she lay awake thinking about how she would deal with the situation. She would talk with Anthony and see if he could find a reason under their agreement why Danny didn't have the power to borrow from a bank. She would talk with Jerry and see if he could find a problem with the loan document. She would talk with Dominic and see if their business would have the cash flow to pay the monthly instalments. And if all else failed, she would have to find another way to pay the bank.

The next morning they drove to work at the usual hour, and while Danny went out on a job Paola made appointments with Anthony for later that morning and with Jerry for that afternoon. She scanned the loan documents and emailed them to Jerry so that he could review them before their meeting. She looked at the budget for the rest of the year, comparing the cash flow with the monthly instalments on the bank loan and concluding that without an infusion of cash from somewhere they wouldn't be able to make those payments. By then she only had time to drive to White Plains for the meeting with her brother.

Anthony listened as she related what Danny had done, sitting across a table from him in a conference room. When she told him Danny still owed money to the mob, he asked: "Do you know how much he owes them now?"

"He said about fifty thousand dollars."

"Well, I hope it's not more."

"Yeah. It wouldn't take much more to put us under."

Anthony looked at her sympathetically as he did years ago when she was a victim of bullying on the street where the kids in the neighborhood played. "So you want to know if I can find a reason under your agreement why Danny didn't have the power to borrow from that bank."

"I know it only takes one signature, but I'm hoping there might be something else."

"Well, I reviewed the agreement after you called, and I did find something, but it's a long shot."

She waited for him to continue.

"There's a clause that addresses the death or the incapacitation of Danny. It provides that in the event of his death his half ownership reverts to you, and that in the event of his incapacitation his powers under the agreement are terminated."

"I remember the part about his death, but I don't remember the part about his incapacitation."

"I added that part."

"You did?" she said. "Did you have any particular reason?"

"Knowing what happened at the electric company, I thought it would be prudent to cover that eventuality. But it's a fairly standard provision."

"So how could we use it?"

"We could claim that Danny was incapacitated because of an addiction."

There was no way her brother could know about Danny's addictions, but just to make sure, she said: "You mean an addiction to gambling?"

"Yeah. I think we have ample evidence that he was addicted to gambling, and that he was affected by this condition long before he went to the bank. So when he signed for that loan, he was incapacitated and therefore his power to borrow money had been terminated."

"Do you think we'd have a chance of winning the case with that argument?"

"I haven't had time to check the precedents, but as I said, I think it's a long shot."

"If we pursued it, what would Danny have to do?"

"He'd have to cooperate. He'd have to admit that he was addicted. And he'd have to submit to a psychiatric examination."

"Would we have to go to court?"

"Oh, yeah. And it would take a lot of time."

"Would you handle the case?"

"Since I'm your brother," Anthony told her, "I'd get someone else to handle it. An attorney who wasn't a member of your family would have more credibility."

She understood. "Well, let me ask you, do you believe that Danny *was* incapacitated when he signed for that loan?"

"Yeah, I believe he was. The guy was desperate. The mob was threatening to hurt his daughter."

"Could we use that threat to prove he was incapacitated?"

Anthony laughed. "How would we prove they made that threat? And who would we bring as a witness?"

"Then we could only use his addiction to gambling?"

"Unless he's addicted to other things."

"He isn't now, but he does have a history of addictions."

"That would help. I mean, it would help if he had addictions *after* you brought him into the business. If he had them before, then they could claim you knowingly took a risk in giving him the power to borrow money."

"Do you think I shouldn't have given him the same powers that I had?"

"I understand why you did it. You wanted to help him. And you're my sister, so I'm not going to judge you. But other people might."

"You mean the people who'd hear my case."

Anthony nodded. "I'll check the precedents and see if there's anything that helps. But in the meantime we need to change the agreement so that Danny no longer has any powers and no longer has any ownership."

"I can see why we have to take away his powers. But why do we have to take away his ownership?"

"Because his creditors could make claims against his half of the business, and that could cause serious problems for you."

"Okay. You can make those changes. Does Danny have to agree to them?"

"Of course. He's a party to the agreement."

"Well, I hope he'll understand why we're doing this."

"If you want, I could help you explain it to him," Anthony offered.

"Thanks. I can explain it to him." She was afraid that Danny would feel she was dumping him, and she hoped she would find the right words to make him see that they were only doing it to protect the family.

As she drove to her office she thought about the possibility of getting out of the bank loan. If they won the case on the argument that Danny had been incapacitated by his addiction to gambling, it would relieve their business of the debt. To pursue this case Danny would have to admit that he was addicted to gambling and he would have to undergo a psychiatric examination, but as much as that could hurt him, it could also help him in the long run, so even if they lost the case they could get something out of it.

She spent the next few hours in her office reviewing jobs and planning for the next day. She could plan ahead for jobs with contractors, but not for the repair jobs that occurred every day and usually had to be scheduled in response to phone calls from people who had lost power in an outlet, a floor, or a whole house. For these jobs she had to maintain some slack in her work force, and she had found that it was most effective to deploy a few floating teams that did nothing but respond to emergencies. Since she was often in the field supervising a major job or mentoring an apprentice on a repair job, she had hired and trained a young woman to handle phone calls and figure out which team could respond the soonest, so she had to keep track of where these teams were and what they were doing. The woman's name was Monica, and she was bilingual which enabled her to handle callers who only spoke Spanish. She lived in Yonkers with her parents, and she could take a bus to the office. While working full time she attended evening classes at St. Catherine in a program that would lead to a master's in early childhood education, so she had little time for partying.

Paola had a daily meeting with Monica that usually lasted from a half hour to an hour, ideally at lunchtime when they could eat tacos from a food truck that served the industrial area. Monica would text an order, and then go out, knowing that by the time she got to the truck her order would be ready. During the fifteen minutes it took her to retrieve the tacos Paola handled the phone calls. Today while Monica was gone Paola got a call from a woman who only spoke Spanish. Though by now she had learned a few words and expressions in Spanish, she had trouble understanding the woman, and she finally had to settle for taking a phone number, which she could do because she knew the numbers one through ten in Spanish. As soon as Monica returned with the tacos Paola gave her the phone number and asked her to call the woman before they started eating.

Monica promptly made the phone call, and Paola listened, trying to follow the conversation. She had much less trouble understanding Monica than the woman, but when the call ended she still didn't know what the problem was.

"What was the problem?" she asked Monica.

"She lost power in her living room. She lives in an apartment, but she says the super's never around, and she needs power so that she can watch her *telenovela*."

"I guess that qualifies as an emergency."

"Yeah, it does. If my grandmother couldn't watch her *telenovela*, she'd drive us crazy."

Paola laughed. "I was following your conversation, and I had much less trouble understanding you."

"I'm Mexican, and she's Dominican. That's why."

"Oh, yeah. I've noticed that when you talk in Spanish with Nelson, you talk a lot more slowly than he does."

"I love Dominicans, but they're different from Mexicans."

"How are they different?"

"They're different in a lot of ways, beginning with how they speak Spanish. They also have different food and music."

"You mean they have a different culture."

"Yeah, they do. I don't think I could marry a Dominican."

"I didn't think I could marry an Irish guy, but I did. And we're still married after nineteen years."

"My mother says that if you really love the guy, it doesn't matter what he is."

"I think your mother's right. I think what matters is having the same values."

When they had finished eating the tacos Paola had time to get to her meeting with Jerry. She found a parking place on Main Street and walked to his office, mindful of the fact that this was the second time Jerry would be dealing with a problem caused by Danny.

The receptionist led her to the conference room, where she waited for Jerry hoping for a legal miracle. But when he entered the room with the loan documents he looked at her with sympathy. When they had sat down at the table he asked: "Now, where did this loan come from?"

"Danny got into debt," she began, and then she paused to clear her throat.

"How did he get into debt?"

"By gambling online."

"Gambling? I hate to ask who he owed the money to."

"He owed it to the mob."

Jerry blew out a puff of air. "Well, he's really done it this time."

"They threatened to hurt our daughter if he didn't pay them, so he went to that bank and got a loan to pay them off."

"You didn't know about it?"

"No, I didn't know about it until I got an invoice for the first instalment."

"He has the power to borrow money on his sole signature?"

"He has all the powers that I have."

Jerry looked as if he questioned her judgment, but he didn't comment. He only said: "So he went to that bank and got a loan and paid off the mob."

"Yeah, that's right. My brother thinks we might be able to claim that Danny was incapacitated when he signed for this loan."

"Incapacitated?"

"By his addiction to gambling."

Jerry considered this. "It's a possibility, but it's a long shot."

"That's what my brother thinks, so I'm hoping you can find another way."

"You mean another way to get out of this loan?"

"Yeah. I looked at the budget of our business, and I don't see how we can repay it."

A light flickered in Jerry's eyes. "You're saying that your cash flow isn't enough to repay the loan?"

"It's obviously not enough."

"Then the bank evidently failed to do the usual due diligence. Did anyone from the bank contact you?"

"No, they never contacted me."

"Then we might have something," Jerry said, flipping the pages of the agreement. "It says that the purpose of the loan was to finance working capital. But you say the purpose was to pay the gambling debt of an owner."

"Yeah, that's what it was used for."

"And you didn't see the transaction because the proceeds of the loan were credited to an account that Danny opened with the bank that made the loan, and the payment to the mob was made from that account. He didn't write a check to them, did he?"

"No. He withdrew the money in cash to pay them."

"If he withdrew ten thousand dollars or more at a time, then the bank would have had to report the transactions."

"I don't know how he withdrew the cash."

"They probably told him how to withdraw it."

"They probably did."

"Okay. I see how he did it without your knowledge. And maybe you can sell the argument that Danny was incapacitated when he signed for this loan, but I think it's a long shot. The only argument I can see now is that the bank failed to do the usual due diligence." Jerry paused. "You may not know it, but that bank made a lot of home mortgage loans that the borrowers had no chance in hell of repaying, and they were nailed by the feds. It made them look bad, and they had to pay an enormous fine, so they could be vulnerable on this issue."

"How would you pursue it?"

"I'd take legal action on behalf of your business claiming that the bank failed to do the usual due diligence in making this loan. I'd cite their failures to do the usual due diligence in making all those mortgage loans. Though I should point out that the people who took those mortgage loans are considered to be unsophisticated, whereas a business is considered to be sophisticated. Of course it depends on the size of the business, and being small works in your favor."

"Do you think it's worth trying?"

"I think it is. I'd do it for you on a contingency basis."

"What does that mean?"

"You only pay my expenses, and if we win I get ten percent of the amount I save you."

"That sounds fine," she said after making a quick calculation. If they saved all that money, then they could afford to pay the contingency fee.

"But I have to tell you, it's a long shot. The main weakness of our argument would be that you're a business, you're not a widow out in the boondocks."

"You could also use the argument my brother suggested—that Danny was incapacitated because of his addiction to gambling, so his power to borrow was terminated."

"That would give us another shot, but they're both long shots."

"I understand. Now, what about the debt to the mob?"

"What debt to the mob?" Jerry asked blankly.

"The additional debt that he incurred while hoping to win enough money to repay the bank."

"Oh, Jesus. You mean he kept gambling?"

"Yeah, he did. He was addicted to it."

Jerry looked at her with sympathy. "To put it mildly, you have your hands full with him."

"I know," she said, refusing to feel sorry for herself. "But he's my husband, and I have to stand by him."

"Up to a point, but you don't have to jump off a cliff with him."

"I won't jump off a cliff with him. Now, what about the debt to the mob?"

"We could claim that they were conducting illegal gambling activities in the state of New York, and we could probably win that case."

"You mean if he'd told me that he was in debt to the mob for gambling, you could have gotten him out of it?"

"I probably could have. But I couldn't have stopped them from hurting your daughter, so don't go too far with that scenario."

She understood. "So if you got him out of this debt, they could still hurt our daughter."

"Yeah, they could. How much does he owe them now?"

"About fifty thousand dollars."

Jerry paused. "If I can get you out of the bank loan, could you pay that amount?"

"I'm sure we could, though we'd have to use all our resources."

"Then I advise you to pay that debt. But you have to stop him from gambling."

"I think I've already stopped him from *that*."

Looking at her closely, Jerry said: "But you don't know if you can stop him from doing something else."

"Well, that's the thing," she said glumly. "I never know what he's going to do next."

"I don't like to get involved in matrimonial matters, but I think you should take measures to protect yourself."

"Protect myself from my husband?"

"Yeah. He might not be hurting you deliberately, but he's hurting you, and if he keeps doing these things he'll ruin your family."

"I know he will. But he's going to have therapy again."

"Again? When did he have therapy before?"

"When he was addicted to opioids. That was the first time."

"You mean he was a drug addict?"

"He was, but not in the usual way. After his accident they gave him painkillers, and he got addicted to them."

"That happens to a lot of people. In fact, it's an epidemic."

"Yeah. I know it is."

"You said his therapy for opioid addiction was the first time. What was the second time?"

"When he was addicted to video games."

Jerry grimaced. "I'm glad he's going to have therapy for his gambling addition, but you're still exposed to the risk of his doing something else."

"He won't be able to do anything else to our business. We're changing the agreement so that he won't have any powers. And we're putting all the ownership in my name."

"What about your house?"

"It's in both our names."

"If he gets into debt again, his creditors could make claims against it, so your house should be in your name alone."

"I understand," she said, seeing the wisdom of this advice.

"So your assets will be protected. But as his wife you could still be liable for his debts."

"I'll take that risk," she said, refusing to abandon him.

That evening after dinner, while Briana was up in her workroom studying, she and Danny went out to the deck. It was early September, and it was still warm enough to sit outside, though after the sun went down there was a chill in the air.

She told Danny about her conversations with Anthony and Jerry, answering his questions as she went along. When she was done he said: "Okay. So what are we going to do?"

"The first thing we're going to do is pay the mob what you owe them now. You said it was about fifty thousand dollars."

"Yeah, fifty thousand. They reminded me today."

"Can you pay them in instalments?"

"I did before. They told me not to withdraw more than nine thousand at a time so the bank wouldn't have to report it."

"How often did you withdraw money?"

"A few times a week."

"Did the bank ever ask you what it was for?"

"No, they were accommodating."

She made a mental note of that, seeing how it would support the argument that the bank failed to do the usual due diligence. "Before you make any commitment, we need to have Dominic analyze our cash flow."

"What about the bank loan?"

"Jerry will try to get us out of the loan by arguing that the bank failed to do the usual due diligence. He says it's a long shot, but it's worth trying."

"What if that doesn't work?"

"Then we'll need to find another way to repay that loan."

"You mean the business can't repay it?"

"I don't see how, but Dominic may see a way."

"What if he doesn't?"

"Then we'll have to sell our house."

"Oh, no," he said as if that would be a total disaster. "Where would we live?"

"We'd find an apartment."

For a long time he was silent, and then he said: "I'm sorry."

She knew he meant it, and she felt bad for him, but she felt worse about what it would do to their family. She didn't know how she would explain it to Briana, but right now she had to explain something to Danny. "We have to change our agreement for the business. We have to take away your power to borrow money."

"I understand."

"We also have to take away your ownership."

"Why do we have to do that?"

"As long as you own half of the business your creditors can make claims against it."

"What creditors?"

"Whatever creditors you might have."

"I won't get into debt again."

"I hope you don't, but I don't want to take that risk."

"You don't trust me?"

"I trust you in most ways, but this is our family business. My father worked his whole life for it."

"I know, but if you take away my ownership, we won't be equal partners anymore."

"We'll be equal partners in our marriage."

"Yeah. But I'll be working for a business owned by my wife."

"I'm sorry if that bothers you," she said, "but if you'd rather work for a business owned by anonymous shareholders, you could get another job."

"I couldn't get another job."

"Why couldn't you?"

"I have a disability."

"That doesn't stop you from doing your present job."

"At times it does. I haven't complained about it, but at times I have pain in my shoulder."

"I'm sorry," she said. "Would you like to work in the office?"

"No. I don't want a desk job."

"Then avoid doing things that cause pain in your shoulder. If you're working with Al or Nelson, they'll understand."

"Okay," he said. "I'll do the best I can."

She believed he meant this statement to be reassuring, but for some reason it had the opposite effect on her.

The next day Dominic, who prepared their financial statements, spent the morning at the office analyzing their cash flow. Being three years older than her, Dominic was closer to her in age than Anthony, who was five years older, but Paola had always been closer to Anthony in other ways, maybe because there had been less competition between them.

Dominic wore silver-rimmed glasses, which made him look professorial, and in fact he taught an accounting course as an adjunct at St. Catherine. The subject was financial statement analysis, which he did for his clients between preparing their quarterly or annual statements. So he was a reliable source of expertise, with the advantage of being a member of the family.

Around noon he came into her office and sat down in front of her desk with somber eyes.

"What do you think?" Paola asked him, sensing the worst.

"I think you were royally fucked by that bank. They're charging you 15% interest, which you could get on a credit card, and they want you to repay the loan over three years, so your monthly payment is $10,399.60."

"That's what their invoice said. Can we pay that much?"

"If your business goes well, and if you and Danny stop taking salaries, maybe you can."

"We live on our salaries."

"I know you do. Could you get them to restructure the loan?"

"What do you mean?"

"Make it payable over ten years?"

"I could ask them," she said, remembering how the manager had treated her. "Does it have to be over ten years?"

"You need at least seven years to have a chance of repaying this loan. And it would help," Dominic added, "if the interest rate was 9%, which you could get from a reputable bank."

"Then why did they make it payable over three years?"

"That's a good question. Maybe they wanted you to default."

"Why would they have wanted us to default?"

"To get their hands on this building. It's worth at least nine hundred thousand, maybe more."

"You think it's worth that much? So could we put a mortgage on the building and use the money to repay this loan?"

"Yeah, you could, but after working his whole life to pay for the building Dad would have a shitfit if you put a mortgage on it."

Weathering his criticism, Paola said: "Okay. We won't try that. Did you imply that this bank isn't reputable?"

Dominic laughed, which he did rarely. "Reputable? The guys who run this bank should be in jail. They're high on the Fed's watch list."

"Well, that should support our argument against them."

"What argument?"

"That they didn't do the usual due diligence when they made that loan to us."

"They didn't at all. If they'd analyzed your cash flow, they would have seen that you couldn't repay this loan in three years."

"Could we use your analysis as evidence?"

"Sure. You can use me as an expert witness."

"But what if we don't win the case? How much *could* we repay the bank over three years?"

After pausing to think her brother said: "About a hundred thousand."

"Then we'd have to reduce this loan by two hundred thousand. But where could we get the money to do that?"

"You could get it from your house."

Paola shook her head, saying: "I don't want to sell our house."

"You might not have to sell it. You have equity in your house, so maybe you could get the money by increasing your mortgage."

"You think we could increase our mortgage by two hundred thousand?"

"I don't know. It depends on the market value of your house. I have a friend who's a real estate agent in your area. She could give you an estimate of its market value."

Paola took the name and phone number of his friend, and they ended the meeting. She didn't feel better, but she didn't feel worse. At least she had a clear idea of where she stood, so she could develop an action plan.

TEN

THAT AFTERNOON, with a copy of the cash flow, she went to the bank for a meeting with the manager. She had scheduled an appointment, but they still made her wait for about a half hour before admitting her to the manager's office.

She sat down in front of him and laid her papers on his desk, saying: "This is the cash flow of our business. It was prepared by our accountant."

The manager moved a hand barely enough to pick up the papers. He glanced at the top paper and asked: "What am I supposed to see in these numbers?"

"You're supposed to see that there's no way we can repay you over three years."

"When we made the loan you were able to repay it. Have you had reversals in your business?"

"No. We're doing fine."

"So what's the problem?"

"The problem is," she said calmly "we can't repay you over three years. We could repay you over ten years, but not over three."

"Is that what these numbers are supposed to show?"

"It's what they do show. If you give us ten years, we won't have any problem."

"Ten years is a long time. A lot of things could happen during that time."

"I know they could, but isn't that a risk you're supposed to take?"

The manager shook his head, saying: "Actually, it isn't. We're not supposed to make loans for longer than three years."

"Are you supposed to make loans that can't be repaid?"

"Are you saying you can't repay us?"

"I'm saying we can't repay you over three years."

"I think you can. We never would have made this loan if we didn't think you could repay it over three years."

Paola looked at him, trying to figure out what might be going on in his mind. He revealed nothing in his cold eyes other than arrogance. "Can you give us seven years?"

"I can't. Our limit for business loans is three years."

Back in her office she took the next step. She called Jerry and told him that the bank manager had refused to extend the period of the loan beyond three years.

"He wouldn't extend the period at all?" Jerry asked.

"No. He said their limit for business loans is three years."

"Do you want to take legal action now?"

"Yeah, I do. And I have something else that might support our case. They allowed Danny to withdraw cash in amounts of nine thousand dollars, a few times a week, and they never asked him what it was for."

"Unless it's ten thousand dollars or more, they don't have to report it. If it had been a construction loan, they would have monitored its progress. But it wasn't a construction loan, it was a loan to finance working capital, which could have been used for anything."

"I also have a cash flow that shows there's no way we can repay that loan over three years. Would that help?"

"Sure, it would help. Who did the cash flow?"

"My brother Dominic. He's a CPA."

"Would he be willing to testify?"

"He said he would."

"Then we'll use the cash flow to support our argument that the bank should have known you couldn't repay them over three years, and that if they'd done the usual due diligence they would have known. But remember," Jerry added, "it's a long shot."

"I understand. Now, what should I do about the invoice they sent me?"

"Don't pay it. If you make a payment they could use it to argue that you accept the validity of the loan, which could undermine our case."

"If I don't pay them, what can they do to me?"

"They can send you another invoice, they can tack on a late fee, and they can take legal action against you, but they can't touch you until they've gone through the legal process, and by then we'll know the outcome of our case."

"Okay," she said, convinced that she had nothing to lose. "Let's go ahead with it."

Next, she found the number of her bank and called them. She asked a young woman to find out how much they had paid down their mortgage. The young woman told her she could get that information online, she only had to go to the website, click on a tab, and follow the instructions. Since she had been given this advice before on other matters, and it hadn't worked, Paola was skeptical, but she agreed to try it.

Finally, she called the real estate agent that Dominic had recommended. The woman who answered wasn't sure if Maddy was there, and asked her to hold while she looked for her. About five minutes later Maddy got on the phone. After several minutes of introductory talk, in which they discovered that they had a mutual friend, Paola gave Maddy the address of her house and asked her if she could do an estimate of its market value. Maddy told her she needed more than just the address of the house, she would need to see it, inside and out, so she agreed to come there at nine the next morning.

That evening she brought Danny up to date on the situation, recounting her conversations with Dominic, the bank manager, and Jerry.

"I got it," Danny said when she was done. "We can't repay the bank over three years, and the bank manager won't give us more than three years, so we're taking legal action."

"Yeah, but remember, it's a long shot."

Danny nodded as if he understood. "Well, the mob has given me three years to repay them."

"What's the monthly payment?"

"About two thousand."

"We could handle that if we didn't have the bank loan, but I don't want to be in debt to the mob, so we need to pay that off." She paused to do some calculations. "My brother says our business could repay a loan of a hundred thousand, so we need to get two hundred fifty thousand to pay down the bank loan and pay off the mob loan."

"Where could we get that much money?"

"We might be able to get it by increasing the mortgage on our house. If we've paid down our mortgage enough, and if the market value of our house has increased enough, then we might be able to get that much. I called the bank to find out how much we've paid down our mortgage, and they told me I could get it from their website. I'll do that later."

"How do we find out the market value of our house?"

"I asked a real estate agent to come here tomorrow and look at the house and give me an estimate of its market value."

After a silence Danny asked: "What if we can't increase our mortgage by two hundred fifty thousand dollars?"

"Then we'll have to sell the house."

"I don't understand how we'd get more by selling the house."

"We'd get our equity, which we wouldn't get by increasing our mortgage."

"Well, I hope we can do it by increasing our mortgage. I don't want to sell the house."

She understood. He didn't want to inflict the loss of her home on Briana, and she didn't either. But she didn't want him to get his hopes up. "The bank will want to see evidence that we can repay a bigger mortgage. And if you think about it, we'd only be moving the loan from our business to our house."

"But if it was a mortgage we'd have thirty years to pay it, wouldn't we?"

"Yeah, we would," she agreed. "And the mortgage rates are favorable now."

"So let's find out how much we've paid down our mortgage."

"I'll do that now—if I can figure out how to do it." She left Danny in the kitchen and went upstairs, where she found Briana on her computer ostensibly doing homework.

"How's it going?" she asked Briana.

"It's going okay. I just finished writing a paper."

"Would you like me to read it?"

"No, not yet. I have to review it and fix some things."

"Could I use your computer for a minute?"

"Sure." Briana got up and started to go.

"I might need some help. Could you stand by?"

"Yeah, sure."

With her daughter's arm against her right shoulder, Paola went to the bank's website, clicked on the tab, and tried to figure out how to get the information, but she was stymied.

"Try clicking on this," Briana said, pointing to an icon.

Paola clicked on the icon, and with further help from her daughter she arrived at a screen where she only had to enter the original amount, the interest rate, and the term of the mortgage. Within a few seconds she found out how much they had paid down their mortgage. She had hoped it would be more.

"What's that number?" Briana asked her.

"It's how much we still owe on our mortgage."

"Mortgage? What's a mortgage?"

"It's a loan you get from a bank so you can buy a house."

"You needed a loan to buy this house?"

"Oh, yeah. Everyone needs a loan to buy a house."

With a furrowed brow, Briana said: "So you owe the bank that much money?"

"Yeah, we do. But we can pay it."

"Well, I hope the bank doesn't take our house."

"Don't worry. They won't."

Apparently satisfied, Briana left the room.

Paola remained at the computer for a while, hoping she had said enough to prepare Briana for what might happen but not enough to upset her. Then she returned to the kitchen, where Danny was still sitting at the table.

"We've paid down about seventy-five thousand dollars," she reported.

"Is that all?" He looked disappointed.

"It's less than I thought, but I remember Dominic saying you mainly pay interest during the first twenty years of your mortgage."

"So how much does the market value have to be?"

"I figure it has to be at least four hundred thousand dollars."

"You think it's that much?"

"I have no idea. I hope it is. But we have to be prepared for whatever happens."

With his eyes closed and tears trickling through his eyelids, he reached for her hand.

The next morning, at five minutes before nine, the doorbell rang. It was a woman with curly reddish hair and greenish eyes, wearing a blue blazer over a white blouse and a gray skirt, which reminded Paola of the uniforms they wore as Catholic school girls.

"Hi, I'm Maddy."

"I'm Paola. Come in." She stepped aside and let Maddy walk by her, realizing that the agent was already checking out the house.

"Are you planning to sell?"

"We're thinking about it," Paola said truthfully. "It depends on the market value."

"Well, the market's good for sellers now. We don't have much inventory."

With Maddy taking notes on a clipboard, Paola showed her the downstairs, the upstairs, and finally the basement. They ended in the kitchen, where Paola made coffee.

Sitting at the table, Maddy said: "There are pluses and minuses. The pluses are the deck, the backyard, and the finished basement. The minuses are that the house has only one full bathroom, two of the bedrooms are a bit small, and the kitchen needs updating. But all in all, it's a good house, and it should sell."

"At what price?"

"In this market you could probably get around four hundred thousand. But that's a guess," Maddy cautioned. "Now that I've seen the house, I can look at comparables and then give you a better idea."

"Okay," Paola said.

They talked for a while about their mutual friend, and then Maddy had to go, responding to a call on her cell phone.

Instead of guessing how much their bank would increase their mortgage, Paola decided it was time to ask the bank to start the process of increasing the mortgage, so after calling her office to let them know she wouldn't be there for another hour, she drove to the bank, which was on Nepperhan Avenue.

Inside, she asked to see a loan officer, and within a few minutes she was sitting in a cubicle with a smartly dressed woman whose hair was held back by a clamp.

"How can I help you?" the woman asked in what sounded like a Jamaican accent. According to a brass plate on her desk, her name was Jasmine Powell.

"I want to increase our mortgage," Paola said.

"Can you give me your account number?"

"I don't have the number, but my name is O'Dwyer, Paola O'Dwyer."

Jasmine did some typing on her computer, and then said: "I have it. You have a checking account, a credit card, and a mortgage with us."

"Yeah, we've been customers for a long time."

"By how much do you want to increase your mortgage?"

"By two hundred fifty thousand dollars."

Jasmine raised her eyebrows slightly. "What will you use the money for?"

"Home improvements."

"Can you be more specific?"

Trying to think of uses for the money, Paola said: "We need a new roof, a new bathroom, and a new kitchen. We need to have the house painted. We need to have the yard landscaped. And we need to have the sidewalks replaced."

"Do you plan to sell the house?"

"No, we just want to improve it. We've lived there for almost eighteen years without doing any major improvements."

"We'll need an appraisal before we can tell you how much you could increase your mortgage. Should I go ahead and get an appraisal?"

"Yeah, go ahead. How long will that take?"

"We should have it within a week or so."

She filled out a form and signed it and left the bank, hoping that the appraisal would be at the level that Maddy had estimated.

On Friday she had drinks with Gabby at O'Malley's. She had offered to bring Danny with her so that he could join his friends at the round table, but he had turned her down. She listened while Gabby told her about the new superintendent that she had to deal with, and then she told Gabby about the loan that Danny had taken without her knowledge.

"So he got addicted to gambling," Gabby said as if she wasn't surprised.

"I had no idea he was gambling," Paola said. "I keep asking myself if there was something I should have noticed, but I can't think of anything."

"Where did he gamble?"

"Down in our basement, on his computer."

Gabby nodded. "Where he got addicted to video games."

"But I couldn't stop him from using his computer."

"I know you couldn't stop him. Danny's not a child, he's an adult. He's responsible for his actions."

"Well, sometimes I wonder if Danny wants to be a child."

"I think all guys want to be children. They want to go back to the time when they didn't have any responsibilities."

"You mean they don't want to grow up."

"When Robert watches a football game he's back in high school, and he's happy to be there for the rest of the evening."

"But he's only addicted to football."

"Yeah, and there's a cure for that addiction."

"There is? What?"

"Losing. His team is the Jets, and they keep losing, so after a while he switches to another channel and watches something else."

"I could live with that. I wish Danny was addicted to sports."

"Be careful of what you wish for. He might get into those football pools. Like the one the guy over there is running." Gabby directed her eyes toward a tall guy at the other end of the bar who was always at O'Malley's. He had a briefcase which he opened and closed discreetly after doing transactions with people.

"Anyway, I hope we can increase our mortgage enough to pay off Danny's debts."

"You only mentioned the bank loan. He has other debts?"

"He has a debt to the same organization that he paid off with the bank loan."

"You mean the mob?"

"That's what he said. He said they threatened to hurt our daughter if he didn't pay them."

"Oh, my god. Are you sure he's stopped gambling?"

"As sure as I can be."

"Is he seeing a therapist?"

"He's seeing the guy who helped him before," Paola said. "But I don't know about therapy. It helped him overcome his previous addictions, but it obviously didn't stop him from getting addicted to something else."

"It didn't get to the root of the problem. Maybe you should give him shock treatment."

"Shock treatment? What do you mean?"

"Tell him that if he ever gets addicted again, you're going to leave him."

"Oh, I couldn't leave him. I mean, he needs help."

"He does need help, but it might not be the kind of help that you can give him."

"But I *love* him," Paola said as a refutation of what Gabby was suggesting.

"I know you love him," Gabby said, reaching over and taking her hand, "but at times it's not enough to love someone."

"If it's not enough, then what does he need?"

"He needs to go deep inside himself and get to the root of the problem. A therapist can help him do that, but ultimately Danny has to do it."

"So how can I help him do it?"

"As I said, you could give him shock treatment. The fear of losing you might motivate him to deal with the problem."

"What do you think the problem is?"

"I don't know. I can understand why kids at our school get into drugs. They're escaping from reality. They have single parents, they live in dangerous neighborhoods, and they have no hope for the future. But Danny has everything. He has a wife, a daughter, and a good job. So I don't know what he needs to escape from."

"Well, maybe he doesn't need to escape from anything. Maybe he needs external stimulation."

"Yeah, he's an extrovert. He gets energy externally. But with all the energy he can get from his family and his friends, he shouldn't have to get it from drugs or video games or gambling."

"Maybe he needs more energy than we can give him."

"Then he should generate more energy from within himself, instead of relying on other people to give it to him."

"You know," Paola said after reflecting. "Each time it's worse. I mean, it has more negative consequences. So I wonder if he's trying to see how far he can go."

"You mean without having to deal with the consequences?"

"Yeah. Every time he gets addicted, I deal with it. He can count on me to deal with it."

"Then you have to make him realize that the next time *he* has to deal with it."

"So I should tell him that the next time he gets addicted I'm going to leave him?"

"That might shock him into realizing what his addictions have done to his family. But it'll only work if he believes you really mean it."

"I understand," Paola said.

As soon as she was on her own, without the immediate support of her friend, she realized that it was easier said than done. When she rehearsed the scene, which she did over and over, she always came to the point where after delivering her ultimatum she saw the reaction in Danny's eyes, the look of a child being rejected, and it made her waver. But then she saw how even if they made it through this crisis, they wouldn't have any resources left for the next crisis. And she dreaded having to go to her father and tell him she had lost the business, she had lost what he had worked for his whole life.

They were sitting in the kitchen after dinner. Briana had gone upstairs to study, so Paola had an opportunity to implement her decision. She began by saying: "We should hear from the bank in a few days. And if the appraisal is high enough, we can pay off our debts by increasing the mortgage. But if we can, I don't want to go through this again."

"You won't," he said. "I promise."

"You've made promises before, but you've broken them, and you've left me dealing with the consequences. You seem to take for granted that whatever you do, I'll deal with it. But what if you couldn't count on me to deal with it?"

"What do you mean?"

"What if I wasn't here for you? Would that stop you from getting addicted again?"

"I don't need that to stop me. I can stop myself."

"I know you *can* stop yourself, but I don't think you want to."

"You think I don't want to stop myself?"

"Maybe you do, but not enough. Or you wouldn't keep getting addicted."

"So what are you saying?"

"I'm saying that the next time you get addicted, *you* will have to deal with it. I won't be here for you. *Capeesh?*"

It was in his eyes, the look of a child being rejected, and it broke her heart. But she didn't waver, she met his look steadfastly.

"Where would you go?"

"I'd go and live with my parents," she said, "and Briana would come with me."

"What about me?"

"You'd be on your own, dealing with the consequences."

He gazed at her as if he was trying to measure her level of determination, and he finally said: "Well, we don't have to worry about that happening."

"I hope we don't," she said, standing firm.

Two days later, as she was in her office planning for the day, Jasmine at the bank called and told her they had the appraisal and asked her if she wanted to discuss an increase in her mortgage. She said she did, and they arranged to meet at eleven.

They went into the same cubicle and sat down. There were papers arranged on the top of the desk, including an official-looking document.

"Not to leave you in suspense," Jasmine said. "They appraised your house at three hundred sixty thousand dollars."

"Is that all?" Paola asked. "But the realtor estimated a market value of four hundred thousand."

"Oh, realtors always estimate on the high side. It encourages people to sell their houses."

"Is the total amount of the mortgage based on the appraisal or on the estimated market value?"

"The appraisal *is* the estimated market value."

"Then how much can we increase our mortgage?"

"You can increase it by a hundred thirty-eight thousand."

"How did you get that number?"

"Well, you can increase your mortgage by the allowed total mortgage, which is eighty percent of the estimated market value, minus the existing mortgage, which is a hundred fifty thousand, and that works out to a hundred thirty-eight thousand."

"When we got our original mortgage, it was ninety percent of the estimated market value. Why is it only eighty percent?"

"Along with other banks, we had a lot of problem loans during the financial crisis. In fact, we had a lot of foreclosures in your area. So now we have a tighter rule on loan-to-value."

"You couldn't bend the rule?"

"I'm sorry," Jasmine said as if she meant it. "I have to follow the bank's policy."

"Well, an increase of a hundred thirty-eight thousand isn't enough," Paola said. "We need an increase of two hundred fifty thousand."

"That's not possible."

"Are you sure?"

"I'm sure."

As she left the bank Paola knew that her only hope of not having to sell the house was to win their legal action against the bank that had made the loan to Danny. She hadn't heard anything from Jerry, but she realized that it would take time, and the longer it took, the longer her hope would be prolonged.

Later that day, she was heartened by a phone call from Maddy, who confirmed her estimate of the house's market value. If they sold their house for that amount, after paying the balance on their mortgage they would have enough to pay off their debts. They would have to find a place to live, but she remembered her parents saying that their current tenants were moving out at the end of the September, so the second floor of their house would be available. But she wasn't ready to ask her mother to save it for her.

Three weeks passed without any further developments. Then she got a call from Jerry, who told her that their case had been rejected. He said he would only charge her for his expenses, which she appreciated.

She had prepared herself for the worst, but she still felt defeated, and it took her a while to pick herself up and deal with the situation. She called her mother and asked her not to rent the second floor of their house to anyone. She said she would explain later.

By the time Danny returned from a job she was ready to give him the bad news, and he took it hard, which she understood because they both knew how selling the house would affect their daughter. They agreed to tell Briana that evening.

As usual, the three of them had dinner in the kitchen, and

before Briana could flee upstairs Paola said: "We have something to tell you."

Briana paid attention.

"The business has a big debt, which they can't repay, and the only way we can save the business is by selling our house."

"What?" Briana said with a look of fear.

"We know you love this house, and so do we, but we have no choice. We get all our income from the business, so if the business went under, we wouldn't have any income."

"You said the bank wouldn't take our house."

"The bank isn't taking our house. We're selling it to pay off a debt of the business."

"Why does the business have a debt?"

She glanced at Danny, not wanting to lie but not ready to tell the whole truth. "They borrowed money from a bank."

"Well, they shouldn't have."

"They shouldn't have, but they did. And now we have to pay off the debt."

After a silence, during which she began to cry, Briana asked: "If you sell our house, where are we going to live?"

"We're going to live with Nonna and Nonno. They have a two-family house, and we can live on the second floor. Your uncles and I lived there when we were kids," she added. "We were very happy there."

"But I don't want to leave my friends."

"You won't be far away. You can walk here."

Briana sat there, staring bleakly into space, and then without another word she got up and left the kitchen.

"That didn't go well," Danny said.

"Well, how did you expect it to go?" Paola said with a flare of anger. "And you just sat there, letting me deal with it."

"I was going to say something, but you said it all."

"She'll blame me, she won't blame you."

"She'll blame us both, but she'll get over it."

"Eventually, yeah. But right now she must feel like the bottom of her world fell out."

"Are you sure we have no choice but to sell the house?"

"The only alternative is to get a mortgage on the building, and I'm not going to do that. My father worked his whole life to pay for that building."

"Have you asked him about it?"

"No, I haven't, and I'm not going to. He trusted me to run the business, and I'm not going to ask him to bail me out."

"What if I asked him?"

"If you did, you'd have to tell him why we need the money. Are you willing to do that?"

Danny hesitated and finally said: "No, I guess I'm not."

"Then forget about the building. We're not going to touch it."

When they were done talking she went upstairs to Briana's room, where she found Briana lying face down on her bed as if she had fallen from a great height. Paola sat on the edge of the bed and gently laid a hand on Briana's back.

"Everything's going to be all right," she said.

Briana said nothing.

"We love you," she said, tenderly kissing Briana's head.

Briana still said nothing.

The next day they signed a contract with Maddy, who listed the house at four hundred thousand. If they got that price they could pay their debts and somehow scrape together enough to pay Maddy's commission and the closing costs.

As the days passed, Briana seemed to become more positive about living in the same house as her grandparents. Paola took her over there and showed her the second floor, where they would live, and showed her the bedroom she would have. It helped that this bedroom was actually bigger than her bedroom in their house.

By the middle of November they had some good offers, and Briana no longer sulked about having to move. It looked as if they could start over with a clean slate.

But then one evening, after returning from a job that had taken longer than it should have, Al came into her office and closed the door ominously.

"What is it?" she asked, sensing a problem.

"He's at it again," Al said unhappily.

"You mean Danny?"

"Yeah. He's like he was before."

"When did you notice?"

"Last week. I was hoping he was just having a bad day, but after today I don't have any doubt about it."

"Where is he now?"

"He's out in the parking lot with the guys."

"Okay. Thanks."

She went out and found Danny telling a story to a group of guys. She waited until he had delivered the punch line, which got a big laugh, and then she told him: "We gotta go."

He looked at her as if he didn't like being interrupted.

Before he could start another story, she said: "Come on."

He turned from the guys, giving them a farewell wave, and joined her.

She didn't say another word until they got into her car, and then she said: "Now, don't give me any bullshit. Are you back on drugs?"

"Yeah," he admitted, staring through the windshield.

"Where are you getting them?"

"From a guy who comes around."

"And how are you paying for them?"

"I have an account."

"You have an account?"

"I have credit with the guy."

"Oh, shit," she said. "You're running up a debt with him?"

"It's not much. It's only a few thousand dollars."

"Exactly how much do you owe him?"

"I don't know. I'll have to ask him."

She rested her forehead against the steering wheel, trying to get ahold of herself. "I told you that the next time you got addicted, you'd have to deal with it, so you have to deal with this situation. I'm not going to deal with it."

"What do you mean?"

"I'm not taking you to a therapist, and I'm not paying your drug dealer. I'm not going to let you ruin my family."

"I'm sorry," he said in a small voice.

"Being sorry isn't enough. You have to do something about your problem."

"What can I do?"

"You can try to figure out why you keep getting addicted to things. You can try to understand why you need these things when you have a wife, a daughter, and a job."

"What if I can't figure it out?"

"You can if you try."

"Well, what if I don't feel like trying?"

"Oh, Danny," she cried, with her heart breaking. "What happened to you?"

There was a long silence, and finally in a voice she barely recognized he said: "I had an accident, and I lost my job. That's what happened."

"You recovered from your injury, and you have another job."

"But I don't love this job the way I loved that job."

"Most people don't love their jobs, but they do them anyway. They suck it up."

"I guess I haven't learned to suck it up."

"Well, you better learn."

"So what are you going to do?" he asked after another long silence.

"I'm going to see Jerry," she said, "and find out how I can stop being liable for your debts."

"You could divorce me. That's the easy way."

"I'm not looking for the easy way. I'm looking for the right way. I have to do what's best for my family."

She started the car and pulled out of the parking lot and headed home, acutely conscious of the fact that it wouldn't be their home much longer.

She was sitting in Jerry's conference room, waiting for him. She hadn't told him what she had in mind because it was too complicated to explain over the phone. But when he appeared she could tell from his face that it wouldn't surprise him.

"He's done it again?" Jerry asked, sitting down.

"Yeah, he's done it again," she said. "I told him that the next time he got addicted, he'd have to deal with it. And he's addicted to drugs again."

"So you're going to let him deal with it?"

"Yeah, but I also want to make sure that whatever he does in the future, I won't be liable for his debts."

Jerry considered. "Well, you wouldn't generally be liable for debts he incurs for things that aren't family necessities."

"What do you mean by necessities?"

"Food, clothing, mortgage payments, utilities—things you need for your family."

"What about drugs?"

"It depends on their purpose."

"I'm talking about opioids," she said. "He says he takes them to relieve pain, but I think he has another reason for taking them."

"In that situation, the drugs could be considered a necessity."

"Then what can I do so I'm not liable for his debts?"

"You can get a divorce."

"Yeah, I know. But is there another way?"

"You want to stay married to him?"

"I do," she said with an echo of her wedding vow.

"I won't ask you why, but I respect your commitment. And luckily there *is* another way. You could get a legal separation."

"What does that mean?"

"It means you're still married but you're legally separated, so you're not liable for each other's debts. But there's a catch."

"What's the catch?"

"You have to live separately. You can't even spend one night with each other or else the arrangement could be questioned."

"What about our daughter?"

"Unless you want to protect her from him, you don't need custody. She can spend whatever time she wants with either of you."

"Could we do things together with her?"

"Oh, yeah. You just have to live separately."

"We're selling our house," she said, wanting him to have the full picture, "and we're going to live with my parents. They have a two-family house. But if we were legally separated, Danny would have to get his own apartment, right?"

"Right. He could live nearby but not with you."

She thought about how Danny would take this, and how Briana would take it. But she knew that if she didn't do it, Danny could ruin her family. And seeing no choice, she said: "Okay. Let's do it."

When she explained the arrangement to Danny that evening he had a lot of questions. In particular, he found it hard to understand why they had to live separately. He kept repeating: "I don't understand why that's necessary."

"It's necessary because if we lived together, we wouldn't be separated."

"We'd be *legally* separated, wouldn't we?"

"It's only legal if we live apart. But you can get an apartment nearby, and you can see us as often as you want. We can even go out together. We just can't spend the night together."

"Could we make love during the day?"

"I didn't ask that question," she said. "I assume we could—if we both wanted to."

He didn't blink. "Well, I don't see how we could afford to pay rent on an apartment."

"We can manage somehow. We just can't afford to pay any more debts."

"There won't *be* any more debts."

"I hope not. Did you find out what you owe them now?"

"Three thousand four hundred thirty dollars."

"We can handle that much, but no more."

"There won't be any more," he said. "Now, when are you going to tell Briana?"

"*We* are going to tell Briana. I want you there to support our getting a separation."

"But I don't want to get a separation."

"Would you rather get a divorce?"

"No. But this will be very hard for Briana."

"It'll be hard for all of us. But at least for me it won't be as hard as losing the business and betraying my father's trust in me."

He sighed. "Okay. When do you want to tell her?"

"The sooner, the better."

They went upstairs and they found Briana in the workroom, pretending to study.

"Honey, we need to talk with you," Paola told her. "It's about something your father and I are going to do."

Briana turned from her computer and faced them with a guarded look.

Since there were no other chairs, Paola sat down on the floor and Danny did likewise. She began by saying: "We need to tell you the whole story about why we have to sell our house. So please listen very carefully."

"You know about the bank loan that we couldn't repay," Danny said. "Well, I took that loan to pay off a gambling debt."

"A gambling debt?" Briana said.

"Yeah. I ran up a debt gambling online, and I couldn't pay it, so I used the business to get the money to pay it off."

"Why were you gambling?"

"For the same reason that I was playing video games. I was addicted to them. In fact," he admitted, "I'm a serial addict. It started with opioids."

"What are opioids?"

"They're drugs to relieve pain. I started taking them to relieve the pain in my shoulder after the accident, and I kept taking them. I got treatment for that addiction, but then I got addicted to video games, and then I got addicted to gambling."

Briana confronted her mother, asking: "Why did you let this happen to him?"

"I didn't know it was happening."

"She couldn't have known," Danny said. "I hid it from her."

"But why did you get addicted to things?"

"I don't know. I'm sorry."

Briana compressed her mouth as if she was suppressing other questions. Then she started to get up from her desk.

"Wait," Paola said. "There's more."

"More?" Briana said, sitting back down heavily.

"Your father stopped gambling, but now he's on drugs again, and he's getting into debt again. If he doesn't stop, we could lose the business. We could lose everything."

"I don't believe it," Briana said, giving her a hard look.

"Tell her," Paola said, appealing to Danny.

"What she said is true," Danny said. "I'm getting into debt again, and if I don't stop, we won't have the money to repay it."

After a silence Briana asked: "So what are you going to do?"

"We're going to get a legal separation," Paola said. "That will protect me and the business from people your father owes money to."

"You're getting a divorce?"

"It's not a divorce. It's a legal separation. We'll still be married, and we'll still see each other. But your father and I can't live together."

"Why can't you?"

"Because if we did, then I wouldn't be protected from people your father owed money to."

"Where will you live?" Briana asked her father.

"I'll get an apartment nearby."

"What about me?"

"You'll live with me," Paola said. "But you can see your father any time."

Briana was silent for a long time, evidently processing the information she had received, and then she asked: "Do I have anything to say about this?"

"Yeah, you do. What do you think?"

"I think it sucks," Briana said, getting up from her desk. Without another word, she left the room and went into her bedroom and slammed the door.

"I told you," Danny said.

"You didn't have to tell me," Paola said. "I knew. It's not a great solution, but the other solutions are even worse."

He didn't comment.

Later, when she went into Briana's room to say goodnight, she found Briana lying face down on her bed in the same position as the last time. But this time Briana quickly turned over and screamed: "I hate you for what you're doing to Dad. I hate you!"

ELEVEN

SHE LEFT BRIANA'S bedroom and returned to the kitchen where she poured herself another glass of wine. She had lost count of how many glasses she had drunk since returning from the house with Briana's clothes, but she didn't feel tipsy, she only felt a deadening effect as she sat at the kitchen table, accepting the fact that the second floor of her parents' house would be her home for the foreseeable future, and that Danny would live in the apartment they had found for him on Palisade Avenue, within easy walking distance. It had two bedrooms, so Briana could spend the night there, which she had done several times since Danny moved there. Paola had seen the apartment only twice: before they agreed to rent it, and before they bought furniture for it. The second time was more than a week ago, so she decided to go there the next day with Briana to see how Danny was doing, and to invite him to spend Christmas Eve with her family.

The next morning, after calling Danny to let him know that they were coming, she had trouble getting Briana out of bed, and the only thing that finally worked was her suggestion that they walk over to her father's apartment. By the time they finally left, it was after eleven. On the way Briana kept looking at her phone as if she was expecting an urgent message from someone, or else as a way to avoid engaging in conversation. Turning onto Palisade Avenue, Paola smelled Chinese food from the restaurant among the various storefronts. The building had four stories with a facing of light brown brick and fire escapes. Its entrance was at the other end, behind a deli. Danny's apartment was on the third floor, and Paola let Briana lead the way up the stairs. At the top she paused to catch her breath, reminding herself that she needed to start an exercise program to get back into shape.

When Danny opened the door for them he didn't look well. By now he had completed the detox phase of his treatment, so he should have looked better than the last time she had seen him, but she thought he looked worse, and she wondered if he was eating properly.

Briana hugged him with more energy than she had shown since getting out of bed, and Paola kissed him on the cheek as if he was a good friend.

"You've lost weight," she told him. "What are you eating?"

"Food from the deli," he said. "They have a line of steam trays every day except Sunday."

"What kind of food do they have?"

"They have everything—fried chicken, beef stew, mac and cheese."

"So you don't have to cook."

"No, I don't even have to warm it up."

"Well, that's good. But I hope you're eating more than one meal a day."

"I am. Don't worry."

They moved toward the living room where Briana had already turned on the television. The arrangement of the furniture reminded Paola of the apartment where Danny had lived when she met him. A sofa in the middle of the room faced the television, with a chair on each side, and not much else. While their daughter became engrossed with a rerun of a crime series they wandered to the window and stood there, looking out.

"How's therapy going?" she asked.

"It's going well. I'm drug free."

"That's good. Do you feel well enough to come back to work?"

"No, not yet. I need more time to get myself together."

"Well, let me know when you're ready."

"I will. But I don't know if I can do the job. My shoulder's killing me, and the only thing I can take for the pain is ibuprofen."

"You should get physical therapy."

"You think it would help?"

"I think it would."

"Then I'll go to that girl who helped me before."

For a while they stared out the window in silence, and then she said: "We're having the usual family dinner on Christmas Eve. I'd like you to join us."

"Oh, no," he said. "I can't face your family."

"They don't blame you. They understand."

"I don't believe it. How can they possibly understand when even I don't understand?"

"They understand enough. And they still accept you as my husband."

"But why do you want to stay married to me?"

"I love you," she said. "I care about you."

"You care what happens to me?"

"Yes, I care what happens to you. That's what I think love is, caring what happens to another person."

"It's also other things, isn't it?"

"Yeah, it's also other things. But I think caring about another person is the heart of it."

"Okay," he said. "If you really want me at your family dinner, I'll be there for you."

"I really want you there," she said, and then she broached the other subject. "This fall semester Briana didn't do her homework. I haven't seen her grades yet, but they won't be good, and that could hurt her chances of getting into the nursing program at St. Catherine. But if she gets good grades in the spring semester, they might think she only had a bad semester, and they might overlook it. So please encourage her to do her homework."

"I will," he said. "I'll get a desk for her bedroom, so she can do her homework there."

"That's a good idea. Whatever she claims, she can't do her homework and watch television at the same time."

"Don't worry. I won't let her try."

When she left the apartment Briana remained there with her father. Paola had hoped that Briana would come with her, but she didn't make an issue of it. She didn't want to subject Briana to any more stress.

For the Feast of Seven Fishes her father put an extra leaf in the dining room table, which her mother set for fourteen people, including Anthony and Dominic, their wives, and their children. Anthony's wife, Emma, was of German descent, and Dominic's wife, Jelena, was of Polish descent, so now they had elements of Irish, German, and Polish in the family. Anthony had three children, and Dominic had two children, and all but one of them were girls, so there was only a single male offspring to continue the family name.

They waited for Danny, but with the children getting restless, her mother had them sit at the table, and she began with the usual prayer. As they were passing the bowls and platters around the table, Paola got up and went into the kitchen and called Danny, but he didn't answer. Hoping that he was on his way, she returned to her place at the table. Though she joined her family in the feast, Paola was conscious of the empty place that her mother had set for Danny.

"I hope nothing happened to him," her mother said as if she had read Paola's mind.

"I hope so too," Paola said. "He said he'd be here."

"In our tradition of celebrating Christmas Eve," Jelena said, "we always set an extra place for an unexpected guest."

"Does he ever show up?" Anthony asked.

"He never did in my family."

"Who is he?" the oldest girl asked.

"I don't know. But he could be a homeless person, or a traveler from far away."

"Could he be Jesus?"

"Yeah, he could be. That's why you set an extra place, so you're ready for him. I mean, so you're not embarrassed by not having a place for him."

"If it *was* Jesus," the girl said, "would he eat the food?"

"Of course he would. He was raised from the dead in the flesh. He ate food with his apostles when he joined them after his resurrection."

Paola was thankful for the conversation because it distracted them from what she was feeling, but as soon as she had helped her mother serve the desert she went into the living room and called Danny.

"Yeah?" he said, answering.

"Where are you?"

"I'm at the bar in the next block."

"You mean Hogan's?"

"I guess." He shouted to someone. "Yeah, it's Hogan's."

"You said you'd be here."

"Well, I was on the way, but I stopped here to fortify myself, and I ended up staying."

"Oh, Danny," she sighed. "I wanted you to be here with my family."

"I'm sorry, but I couldn't face them."

It was too late for him to join them, and in any case it wouldn't have helped his standing in the family to show up in his condition. "Have you eaten anything?"

"No, I haven't. I've just been drinking."

"I'll ask Briana to bring you some food. Okay?"

"Okay. I'll wait for her here."

"You should go to your apartment and wait for her there."

"Oh, yeah," he said as if he understood. "I'll go there as soon as I finish this drink."

When her brothers and their families had gone she found two aluminum containers that her mother had saved from taking home leftover restaurant food, and she put seafood into one and pasta into the other, covering them with aluminum foil.

"Would you take this food to your father?" she asked Briana, who was sitting in front of the television.

"Yeah, sure," Briana said, her face lighting up. "Where is he?"

"By now he should be at his apartment."

"Did you invite him to join us?"

"Of course. Who did you think we set the extra place for?"

"I thought it was for a homeless person, or for a traveler from far away."

"That's what your Aunt Jelena said. She was telling us about a tradition in the Polish culture."

Briana frowned. "If you invited him, then why didn't he show up?"

"I guess he felt he wasn't wanted."

"That's sad," Briana said with deep sympathy for her father.

"It *is* sad," Paola said, holding back tears.

"Oh, why can't we all live together?"

Finding what she thought was an apt analogy, Paola said: "Imagine you and me in a boat, out on the ocean, and the boat can only hold two people. If another person gets into the boat, it'll capsize and sink, and all of us will go down with it."

"You mean if we all live together, we won't survive?"

"We might survive, but we might not."

"You don't want to try?"

"I did try. And I'm still trying. If all goes well," she added, "we can all live together again. But not now. Your father needs time to get himself together."

"Tell me how I can help him."

"For one thing, you can help him by doing your homework."

"How will that help him?"

"By helping you, it will help him."

"It will? But why?"

"Because he loves you and cares about you."

Briana nodded. "Okay. I'll do my homework this semester, and I'll get better grades."

Paola kissed her on the forehead and sent her off.

Two weeks later Briana started the spring semester, the last semester of her senior year, and for a while she went to her room after school and did her homework. That lasted until the end of January, and then she stopped spending time at her desk and instead spent time lying on her bed with her laptop. She stopped going to church, refusing to get out of bed in time for the noon mass. She stopped doing her laundry, and by the end of February there were piles of dirty clothes in her room, which began to smell like an animal cage. And she spent more time with her father. Before, she had mostly seen him on weekends, but now sometimes she went to his apartment directly after school and spent the night there. One time, after spending the night there, she went to school directly from there, and when she came home Paola confronted her in the kitchen, saying: "Did you do your homework yesterday."

"Yes, I did," Briana said, averting her eyes.

"What else did you do?"

"I watched television with Dad."

"Did you have any dinner?"

"We had mac and cheese from the deli."

"You had your books with you, so you could have done your homework."

"I did do my homework," Briana insisted.

"For how long?"

Briana shrugged. "I don't know. An hour or so."

"And that was long enough to do your assignments?"

"Yeah, it was. I'm not a dumbo."

"I know you're not. In fact, you're an intelligent girl, and you were always a good student. But after what happened last fall, I want to make sure you're doing your homework."

Briana was silent, and then she asked: "What if I'm not doing my homework?"

"If you're not, then you won't get better grades than you got last fall."

"Why do I have to get better grades?"

"So you can get into a nursing program."

"Well, I don't know if I want to be a nurse."

Surprised, Paola said: "It was your idea to be a nurse, so it's okay if you change your mind. There are a lot of other things you could be. But why don't you know if you want to be a nurse?"

"Because everything has changed."

"Everything hasn't changed. You have the same mother and father, who are still married and still love each other. The only thing that's changed is that we're not living together."

"Why can't we live together?"

Paola took a deep breath. "I explained why we can't live together. If we did, and if your father got into debt again, we could lose the business."

"But you could get another job."

"That's not the point. Your grandfather worked his whole life for that business. Imagine how he'd feel if we lost it because of your father's addictions."

"He's not addicted to anything now."

"He's not now, but he could get addicted again."

"But he says he won't get addicted again."

"He said that before."

"Well, he means it now."

"If he does mean it," Paola said, "then we can live together. But let's see."

"Okay," Briana said hopefully.

"Now, what about your homework? Are you doing it?"

"No. I'm not doing it."

"You were doing it for a while, but then you stopped. Did something happen?"

"No, nothing happened?"

"Then why did you stop?"

"I don't see any point in doing it."

"I told you it would help your father."

"I know, but I don't think it does help him. What helps him is my being with him, and if I'm doing my homework, I'm not with him."

"From what you said, it sounds like you only watch television with him."

"But it's something we can do together."

"You can watch television together, but you also have to do your homework. You can't just watch television."

Briana said nothing.

"And you have to do your laundry. Your room is full of dirty clothes. I'm surprised you have anything clean to wear."

"I'll do it today."

"You could do it now while I'm making dinner."

Without further argument Briana left the kitchen and went to get her dirty laundry.

Despite the positive elements of this conversation, Paola was still concerned about her daughter. In particular, she was concerned about Briana's apparent lack of motivation, which she couldn't help attributing to the influence of Danny, who might have been encouraging Briana to do her homework but wasn't setting a good example. He still hadn't come back to work, and it looked like he might never come back. His behavior made Paola recall how she had to give him a half ownership of the business in order to convince him to work for it, and now that he no longer was an owner, he evidently didn't want to work for a business owned by his wife.

After lying awake thinking about it Paola decided to make an appointment with the therapist that Gabby had recommended, and the next morning, after Briana had left for school in a clean uniform Paola called Janice Healy. An answering service took her message, and an hour later Janice called her back and agreed to meet with her on Thursday at eleven in the morning.

Janice's office was in Hastings, in a commercial building that looked as if it had been built without an architect. The building had no elevator, so Paola climbed the stairs to the third floor, pacing herself because she didn't want to arrive out of breath.

There was no name on the door, and since there was no buzzer or bell, Paola opened the door and went into a waiting room that had a big sofa, two chairs, and a floor lamp. There was none of the usual reading material, not even an old newspaper, and wondering how Janice would know she was there, she didn't sit down, she just stood there in front of the sofa.

A few minutes later the door to an inner office opened, and a stout woman in a navy blue suit appeared in the doorway. She had wiry gray hair and keen blue eyes. "I'm Janice. If you're Paola, please come in."

"I'm Paola," Paola said, advancing toward the doorway.

"It's nice to meet you," Janice said, shaking her hand.

She followed Janice into the office and sat down on a sofa while Janice took her position in a swivel chair. She imagined Janice working with a family, swiveling back and forth in this chair from mother to daughter.

"So Gabriella recommended me," Janice said with a half-smile. "And you must trust her, or you wouldn't be here."

"We've known each other since we were in kindergarten," Paola said.

"I met her as a student at St. Catherine. Did you go there too?"

"Yeah, but I went later. I majored in business."

"I guess that's why I don't remember you as a student."

"I only took the basic course in psychology."

"Well, tell me about your situation."

"How much time do I have?"

"As much as you need. My next appointment isn't until this afternoon."

In as few words as possible she told Janice the history of her family and her marriage. Among the events, she focused on Danny's accident and his behavior since then. And she expressed her concerns about Briana.

When she had finished, Janice said: "Let's talk about Danny. From what you said, Danny was happy until he lost his job."

"Yeah, he was happy until then."

"So he was a lineman for the electric company."

"He was a lineman. That's who he was."

"I understand. His job defined him."

"It did define him. And when he lost it he lost who he was."

"That happens to a lot of people. Their jobs define them, so when they lose their jobs they lose their identities."

"He got a job with our family business, and he liked it, but he didn't love it."

"It sounds like he had trouble adapting to change."

"Oh, yeah, he did. He wouldn't take a management job with the company. He insisted on having his old job back. But with his disability he couldn't do that job anymore."

"He's not unusual in that respect. A lot of men have trouble adapting to change."

"A lot of men? What about women?"

"Women don't have as much trouble adapting to change. We've been adapting all our lives."

"I guess we have. But I wish I could help him learn to adapt."

"Well, if he isn't willing to learn, then you can't help him." Janice paused, and then asked: "What's he doing now?"

"He's doing nothing. He stays up all night watching television or playing on his computer, and he sleeps all day."

"Is he done with his treatment?"

"He's still seeing his therapist, but he's drug free now."

"So why hasn't he gone back to work?"

"I think he doesn't want to."

"Do you think he cares about his family?"

"I think he does, but a lot of the time he acts like he doesn't. I mean, if you'll excuse the expression, he acts like he doesn't give a shit."

"I'm not a nun anymore," Janice reminded her.

"I think he cares about our daughter, but he's not setting a good example for her. In fact, I think he's leading her astray."

"Let's talk about your daughter. What's your main concern about her?"

"My main concern is her lack of motivation. She always wanted to be a nurse, but now she doesn't know if she wants to be one. She always did her homework and got good grades, but now she doesn't do her homework, and last fall she almost failed. When she's with her father, all they do is watch television together. She thinks she's helping him because she's doing something *together* with him. But if that's all they do together, she's only keeping him company."

"It sounds like she's following his example."

"That's what children do, isn't it? They follow the examples of their parents."

"Some do, and some don't. When there's a difference between

their parents, some follow the example of their mothers and some follow the example of their fathers."

"She's not following my example. In fact, she says she hates me for what I did to her father."

"What does she think you did to her father?"

"She thinks I made him live apart from us for no good reason."

"Have you explained to her why you have to live apart?"

"I've explained it more than once, and I think she understands it, but at the same time she refuses to accept it."

Janice nodded. "I assume you can see how your separation would be hard for her."

"Oh, yeah. But it's hard for all of us. It's hard for him."

"What about you? Is it hard for you?"

"It's very hard for me," she said, giving way to tears. "I still love him. I still want to spend my life with him."

"I understand."

She wiped her eyes, appreciating the support. "I've told Briana more than once that if he stops getting addicted to things, we can live together again."

"Does she believe that?"

"I think she does. But it's not now, it's in the future, and you know how kids are. They want everything now."

"I know. I work with students her age."

"My worst fear is that she'll follow her father's example all the way. I mean, that she'll do nothing and care about nothing."

"That's a deadly sin," Janice said with sorrow in her eyes. "It's called *acedia*, which means not caring. It's usually translated as sloth, or laziness, but those words don't capture its full meaning. It's a darkness of the soul, an indifference to God."

"An indifference to God," Paola repeated. "She stopped going to church with me."

"When did she stop?"

"About a month ago. We always went to church together."

"Did her father go with you?"

"He did until he lost his job, and after that he only went on Christmas and Easter, but now he doesn't go at all."

"It sounds like your daughter's following his example. By not going to church she's taken a step away from God. She's showing indifference."

"She's almost in the same place as he is."

"I'm glad you said 'almost.' It means you have hope."

"I do have hope. I have hope for him too. But I think I have a better chance with her."

"You should. She's younger."

"So what can I do to help her?"

"You can get her to come and talk with me," Janice said. "I can take it from there."

"Okay. I'll try. And thanks for listening."

"Don't thank me. This is my job. But just so you know, I care about my patients. I care about you, and even though I haven't met them yet, I care about your daughter and I care about your husband. And I agree that there's hope for him, but we should begin with your daughter. If we can help her, then maybe she can help him."

"That's what I'm hoping," Paola said.

She left the office feeling better, though she knew it would be a challenge to get Briana to come and talk with Janice.

When Paola got home from work that evening she found Briana in her room, sitting at her desk, evidently doing her homework. She waited until Briana stopped typing, and then she said: "I saw a therapist today."

"What therapist?"

"The one we talked about before Christmas."

"How did it go?"

"I think it went well. I think it was helpful." Paola paused. "Remember, you said you'd see her if I saw her first."

"I did?"

"You did. So tell me which afternoons next week would work for you, and I'll make an appointment for you."

"Okay," Briana said begrudgingly.

After giving Briana two days to determine which afternoons

would work for her, Paola asked her when she could make an appointment for her. Briana was lying on her bed, playing with her phone, stroking the screen without a purpose.

"I'm not going to see her," Briana told her.

"You promised that you'd see her if I saw her first."

"I didn't promise, I only said I would. And I've changed my mind."

"Can you tell me why?"

With most of her attention on her phone screen, Briana said: "Dad said it would be a waste of time, and he should know."

"Why should he know?"

"He's been seeing therapists for years, and it didn't help him."

"It helped him overcome his addictions."

"Maybe it did, but it didn't stop him from getting addicted over again."

"Is that what he told you?"

"Yeah," Briana said, tapping her phone screen.

Paola didn't know who angered her more, Danny for telling Briana such things or Briana for continuing to play with her phone. Addressing the more immediate problem, Paola said: "When you're talking with someone, you shouldn't be playing with your phone."

"I can do both at the same time."

"No one can do more than one thing at the same time, at least not well. So put it away and pay attention."

Briana slid the phone under her pillow and faced her with mild defiance.

"Therapy can help us. It can't solve our problems, but it can help us solve our problems."

"Well, I don't have a problem."

"I think you do. You're setting yourself up for a crash, and I don't want that to happen to you. So please tell me which afternoons would work for you."

"Any of them would," Briana said, reaching under the pillow for her phone.

The next morning Paola made an appointment for Briana for the following Tuesday after school. And then she called Danny, who answered: "Yeah?"

"You're not helping the situation," Paola told him.

"How am I not helping?"

"By telling Briana it would be a waste of time to see a therapist."

"It was a waste of time for me."

"Maybe, but she's not you. She has her own problems."

"I haven't noticed any problems."

"Then you're not paying attention to her. Maybe you should do something with her besides watching television."

"She likes watching television."

"I'm sure she does. It enables her to escape from reality."

"Well, I didn't create the reality that she wants to escape from."

"Is that what you tell her?"

"I don't have to tell her. She already knows."

"Listen, Danny. If you care about her, you'll encourage her to see this therapist, and you won't say things that undermine what I'm trying to do."

"What are you trying to do?"

She almost said she was trying to stop Briana from following his example, but she only said: "I'm trying to help her."

"I'm trying to help her too. But as you say, she has her own problems. At her age everyone has problems. In fact, it's normal for teenagers to have problems."

"Yeah, but she's being self-destructive."

"You mean by hanging out with me?"

"By doing nothing, by not caring."

He was silent for a while, and then he said: "You think she got that from me?"

"I don't know. What do you think?"

"I think she got it from our situation."

"So we should live together again, and we should pretend there's no problem?"

"But that's her only problem—our separation. If we lived together, it would solve her problem."

"I didn't mean *her* problem, I meant *your* problem."

"Well, I'm drug free now."

"But you still haven't come back to work."

"If I come back to work, will you agree to live together?"

After thinking hard about it she said: "Come back to work, and if you haven't gotten addicted to anything for six months, we can talk about living together."

"Okay," he said as if they had a deal.

The next day he came back to work, and she assigned him to a job with Al. According to Al, he did a good job, and he showed up for the rest of the week. But the following Monday he didn't show up. From the evidence that Paola saw when she came home from work that night, Briana had come home from school, changed from her uniform into casual clothes, and gone to her father's apartment. She called Danny just to make sure that Briana was there, and when Briana answered the phone she reminded her of her appointment the next day at three thirty. She offered to take her to Janice's office, but Briana said she could get there by herself. Though she was heartened by this display of independence, she wondered if Briana had a reason to avoid being taken by her mother to a therapist.

The next morning, shortly after nine, she was in her office when a woman from Sacred Heart called to ask why Briana hadn't come to school. She lied and told the woman that Briana wasn't feeling well, and then immediately she called Danny. She let it ring ten times, and still there was no answer. On the chance that she had misdialed the number, she called again, and she let it ring twenty times.

With her stomach churning with fear, she raced out to her car and drove as fast as she could to Danny's apartment. She found a parking place, entered the building, and climbed the stairs. Since he didn't have a bell, she banged on his door. But there was no answer. She banged on this door again and again, until a man in an undershirt appeared in a doorway across the hall.

"He's probably not home," the man said.

"I know he's home," Paola told him. "Is there a super in this building?"

"He lives in the basement, but if he's not there you might find him out in back."

She went down the stairs to the basement and rapped on a door that said: "Super."

A big man with heavy jowls opened the door.

"I need to get into my husband's apartment," she told him.

"Who's your husband?"

"Danny O'Dwyer."

The man's face brightened. "You mean the storyteller?"

"Yeah, that's the guy. It's very urgent. Something might have happened to him."

The man got the message, fetched his keys, and followed her back up the stairs. She stood aside while he unlocked the door, but she didn't wait for him to enter. She rushed by him into the living room, where she saw Danny slumped on the sofa.

Since she didn't expect to get any information out of him, she ran into Briana's bedroom and found her evidently sleeping. She went to the bed and took Briana's arm and shook it, saying: "Briana, wake up."

But the girl didn't move. With increasing fear, Paola leaned over and made sure that Briana was breathing, and then she shook her arm again. But the girl still didn't move.

"Oh, my god," she said, believing that her daughter was in a coma. She got out her phone and dialed 911 and gave them the information they needed. While she was waiting for them to arrive she went back to the living room, where Danny was slowly rousing himself.

"What the fuck happened?" she asked him furiously.

"What do you mean?" he asked, rubbing his eyes.

"Your daughter's in a coma. Did you give her some drug?"

"I swear I didn't," he said, straightening up. "She must have taken it herself."

"So you're back on drugs? Don't lie to me."

He nodded. "Yeah. I'm back on drugs."

She didn't have time to ask why, she only needed to know: "What drugs?"

"Opioids," he said. "Last night I took some fentanyl, and after I passed out she must have found it and taken it."

"You goddam fucking asshole! You might have killed her." She turned and went back into the bedroom, where she tried again to wake Briana without success.

Within a few minutes she heard heavy footsteps coming up the stairs, and she went to the door and opened it for two big guys. The super had discreetly left as if he didn't want to be seen among such lowlifes.

"The girl's in here," she said, heading for the bedroom.

One of the guys had a stretcher, prepared for anything and probably not wanting to go down all those stairs and come up them again.

She stood by and watched as the younger guy attended to Briana, methodically taking her vitals.

"It looks like she took an overdose," he said. "Do you know what it was?"

"I think it was fentanyl."

"That's bad shit. Come on," he said to his partner, "let's get her to the emergency room."

"What hospital?" she asked.

"St. John's. It's the nearest one."

She stood by while they gently arranged Briana on the stretcher, and she followed them out, marveling at how they were able to take her down the stairs. When they had closed the door of their van she turned to go and get her car. She almost bumped into Danny, who was standing behind her.

"I'm sorry," he said with tears streaming.

"You should be sorry. Why are you on drugs again?"

"I don't know. I guess I couldn't handle the situation."

"Well, if she survives, I'm getting a protective order so you can't see her again. It's bad enough what you did to our marriage, but what you did to her—" She didn't have words to express her feeling. "God damn you!"

She left him and went to her car and drove to St. John's, where she found a place in the visitor's parking lot. She went to the emergency room and let a girl at the desk of the waiting area know she was there for Briana O'Dwyer.

And then she waited for what seemed like eternity.

As much as she blamed Danny, she blamed herself for not doing whatever it took to help Briana avoid this disaster. There must have been something she could have said, or could have done, that would have made a difference. She imagined how Briana, after seeing her father escape from reality with the help of that drug, might have wanted to follow him wherever he had gone. And knowing nothing about the drug, she had taken too much.

She was jolted out of her thoughts by a man in a white lab coat, standing before her.

"Are you Mrs. O'Dwyer?" he asked her.

"Yeah," she said, looking up at him anxiously.

"I'm Dr. Young. Your daughter's going to recover. But she had a very bad overdose, so we'll have to keep her here overnight."

"Is she conscious now?"

"She's more or less conscious. She doesn't seem to remember what happened." The doctor paused. "It was fentanyl. Do you know where she got it?"

"She got it from her father," Paola blurted out, immediately regretting it.

"Her father *gave* it to her?"

"She took it from him without his knowledge."

"You know, we're supposed to report this to the police."

"Please don't report it. We'll deal with it."

"Okay. But if her father's using that drug," Dr. Young said definitively, "you should keep your daughter away from him."

"I know, and I will from now on."

"Well, they're taking her to a room now. You can find out at the desk which room it is, and you can go and see her."

"Thanks," she said. When he had gone she said a prayer of thanks to the Blessed Mother, followed by a petition that they all learn from this experience.

She found Briana in a room with another patient, an old woman who was staring bleakly at the ceiling. Briana still looked like she was sleeping.

Paola drew a chair up to the bed and watched her for a while, feeling grateful to have this child. And then she gently shook Briana's arm.

"What?" Briana said, opening her eyes. "Where am I?"

"You're in the hospital."

"Why am I here?"

"You took a drug, an overdose."

"I don't remember taking it."

"Well, you did take it. They found it in your system. The doctor says you're going to recover, but this should be a lesson for us."

"A lesson? What lesson?"

"That we have to care about each other."

"I care about Dad," Briana said, "and I care about you."

"But you also have to care about yourself. What happens to you happens to us. Because we love you. So if you love us, you have to care about yourself.'

Briana nodded, though at this point she was probably still too groggy to understand.

Paola knew she would have to go over this lesson again, and again, and again until they all learned it. Hoping they would, she took Briana's hand and held it.

TWELVE

BRIANA MISSED A week of school, but with the help of her teachers she was able to catch up, and from then on she did her homework dutifully. But her attitude suggested that she was working without a purpose, doing her homework only because she was supposed to. She was strictly prohibited from going to her father's apartment and hanging out there, though he could come and see her whenever he wanted. Paola had gotten him to agree not to let Briana into his apartment by threatening a protective order against him.

Briana didn't protest this restriction, and Danny went along with it. As soon as he completed another detoxification program he started having dinner with them every Saturday, which gave Briana an opportunity to see him and gave Paola an opportunity to make sure he had at least one good meal that week. With this routine established, Briana reverted to her behavior before the separation: she had dinner with her parents, and then she excused herself and went to her room and played with her phone. She acted as if she was pretending that the family was together again, and that nothing had changed.

One Saturday early in April, as they were lingering at the table after Briana's departure, Paola raised the subject of Briana's lack of motivation, saying: "I'm worried about her. She's doing her homework, but it looks like she's just going through the motions."

"How are her grades?" Danny asked.

"They're not bad. I mean, considering that she missed a week of school. But they could be better. And if she wants to get into a nursing program, they should be better."

"Does she still want to be a nurse?"

"The last time we talked about it, she said she didn't know if she wanted to be a nurse. And that's okay. At her age she doesn't have to know what she wants to do with her life. I just wish she wanted to do something."

"What about her friends?"

"She hasn't seen them for a while. In fact, she hasn't seen them since we moved here. They're only a few blocks away, but she acts like they're in another country."

"It's all my fault," Danny said morosely.

"Instead of saying that to me," Paola said, "you could say something to her that encourages her. I mean, tell her how much you loved being a lineman."

"Oh, I can't see her as a lineman."

"I'm not suggesting that you encourage her to be a lineman. I'm suggesting that you tell her how great it is to love doing something—anything."

He nodded. "Okay. I understand. Can I ask you something?"

"Yeah, sure." She waited, unable even to guess what it might be.

"Do you love what you're doing?"

She thought about it. "I feel good about what I'm doing. I'm running a business that employs people, and the business performs an important service, so it gives me satisfaction. But do I love it the way you loved being a lineman? No, I don't think so. And maybe it's better that I don't love it that way."

"You mean if you lost it," Danny said, "it wouldn't be the end of the world."

"It wouldn't for me, but it would for my father."

"So you're doing it for your father?"

"I'm doing it for my family."

He smiled. "Yeah. You're Italian, so your family's everything."

"But you're my husband. You're included in my family."

"I don't always feel included. When you and your parents and your brothers get together, I feel like the odd man out."

"I'm sorry," she said, recalling how she had felt growing up in a mainly Irish neighborhood. "I wonder if Emma and Jelena feel that way."

"I'm sure they do."

"Then you should join us the next time we get together. You could talk with them about it. You could form a coalition."

He smiled again. "A coalition against the Borgattis."

"Well, I'm in favor of anything that helps you. And getting back to Briana," she told him, "please tell her how much you loved being a lineman."

"Okay. I will."

The next day she managed to rouse Briana in time for the noon mass, and they joined her parents at St. Brigid in the usual pew. Her father always sat at the aisle, and she sat next to her mother, with Briana to her left. During the mass she was aware of Briana sitting or standing or kneeling next to her, and she couldn't help feeling that Briana was only doing the responses and saying the prayers because she was supposed to, just as she did with her homework.

The next morning, after Briana had left for school, she called Janice and made an appointment for Briana on Thursday at three thirty. After getting home from the hospital she had called Janice and told her why Briana had missed her appointment, and their conversation had fortified her for helping Briana recover.

This time Briana, evidently chastened by her reason for missing that appointment, didn't object to seeing Janice, and on Thursday afternoon Paola picked her up at school and drove her to Hastings. She introduced Briana to Janice and sat in the waiting room for about an hour while the two of them talked. She had agreed that they should talk without her at least for the first few sessions and then talk together.

When Briana came out she looked more relaxed than before, and as soon as they had left the building Paola asked her: "How did it go?"

"It went okay," Briana said in a barely audible voice.

"Do you like her?"

"Yeah."

"Do you want to see her again?"

A pause. "Could I see her once a week?"

"Sure. Whatever you want. And I'm going to see her again."

They were walking to the car. "Will you talk about me?"

"Of course we'll talk about you. But that's fair. You talked about me, didn't you?"

"Yeah. We also talked about Dad."

Wanting to respect Briana's privacy, she didn't ask what they had talked about. But after a silence Briana said: "We talked about his addictions."

"I'm glad you did. You know, you can talk with her freely about anything."

"Yeah, I know. We talked about why he keeps getting addicted to things, and I told her I think it's because he doesn't care about himself."

"He acts like he doesn't. Do you think he cares about us?"

"I think he does, and that's why he feels bad when he does something that hurts us."

"So you think he has a conflict?"

"Yeah. I think he doesn't care about himself, but I think he *does* care about us, so he gets addicted to escape from that conflict."

Deeply impressed, Paola asked: "Did you ever consider being a psychologist?"

"Oh, I don't know. But I do want to help people, and that would be a way of helping people."

"Well, you have time to think about it."

They got into the car, and they didn't talk for a while. Then Briana said: "Can Dad go back to work with you?"

"Sure, he can—if he wants to."

"I think he wants to, but I don't know. I'll ask him. Okay?"

"Okay," Paola said, thankful that her daughter wanted to do something positive to bring about a reconciliation. It was better than blaming everything on the separation.

The next day after work she met Gabby at the usual place. As they sat at the bar drinking white wine, she let Gabby talk about her family first, and then she brought Gabby up to date on the latest developments.

"Oh, my god," Gabby said when she heard about the overdose. "Briana's lucky to be alive."

"I know she is. But I don't know if she understands that."

"Kids at that age take life for granted. But she *is* lucky. Do you know how many people are dying of overdoses?"

"No. How many?"

"Thousands of people. More than the number of people being killed in car accidents. And fentanyl! It's the worst. What was Danny thinking?"

"He wasn't thinking."

Gabby shook her head reprovingly. "Do you think Briana had any idea what she was doing?"

"I think she just wanted to do whatever her father was doing."

"So you're not allowing her to go to Danny's apartment."

"I can't," Paola said. "He says he's off drugs, but I never know, and we might not be so lucky the next time."

"You might not be," Gabby said.

After taking a sip of wine Paola said: "Briana saw Janice, the therapist you recommended, and I think it went well. She likes Janice."

"That's good. I've sent a lot of girls to her."

"After seeing her, Briana had an insight that amazed me. She thinks Danny doesn't care about himself, but he cares about us, so he has a conflict, and he gets addicted to escape from that conflict."

Gabby considered this. "Yeah, that makes sense."

"When I saw Janice she talked about *acedia*, which I never heard of before. Have you?"

"No. What does it mean?"

"It means not caring. She said it's a deadly sin, what we call sloth, but it's more than that. She said it's a darkness of the soul, an indifference to God."

"Remember, Janice was a nun, so she has a religious perspective. A psychologist would call it depression."

"But don't they treat depression with drugs?"

"Psychiatrists do, but drugs only treat the symptoms. They don't treat the problem."

"How do you treat the problem?"

"With cognitive behavioral therapy. That's what Janice is doing with you and Briana."

"Then Danny should talk with Janice."

"Yeah, he should. At some point you should all talk with Janice together."

"I think she plans to have us do that, but first I had to get Briana to talk with her."

Gabby sipped her wine and then asked: "What's Danny doing now?"

"He's not doing much. He completed another detox program, and Briana says he wants to come back to work. But he's not doing things he did before. He doesn't come here and hang out with his friends. He goes to Hogan's and drinks alone."

"Hogan's? Remember?" When they were only about nineteen they went there hoping to get served, and the bartender laughed at them, along with all the men at the bar. At the time they felt the men were laughing because they were girls, not because they were obviously under the legal drinking age.

"It makes me sad to think of him there."

"Do you understand what happened to him?"

"Well, thanks to Janice, I understand one thing. I understand that Danny was defined by his job as a lineman, and when he lost that job he lost his identity."

Gabby nodded. "That's happened to a lot of men. I mean, all those men who had jobs in manufacturing or in coal mining. They spent their lives building cars or mining coal, and when they lost their jobs they lost their identities. And they won't settle for anything else. They want their old jobs, and no matter what facts are presented to them, they refuse to believe that those jobs are never coming back."

"That's Danny. No matter what the doctors told him about his disability, he refused to accept that he couldn't have his old job. And he didn't like being a mere electrician."

"But if he wants to come back to work, at least he's willing to give it another try."

"Yeah," Paola said, "and maybe this time he'll like it."

Danny came back to work on Monday, and since Al was taking a few days off to support his wife through her surgery for breast cancer, Paola assigned Danny to Nelson, remembering how well they had worked together on that major project.

At the end of the day Nelson came into her office and sat down in front of her desk as if he had more than a few words to say.

"How did it go?" Paola asked him.

"It went fine. If you want to keep assigning him to me, I'll be glad to have him. He works well, and he entertains me with his stories."

Paola smiled. "He's good at telling stories."

"He told me you had a good time at Punta Cana."

"Yeah, we did. It was one of the best times we ever had."

"He told me you're thinking about going back there."

She hadn't mentioned this possibility to Danny, so Briana must have suggested it to him, hoping they could go there as a family and relive their happy experience. "Yeah, I was thinking of going somewhere for spring break."

"Well, don't go to Punta Cana. It's a nice place, but it's not the real DR. You should go to a place where you can get to know the real DR."

"Can you recommend a place?"

"Yeah. My hometown. It's Santa Cruz, on the north coast, west of Puerto Plata."

"What's there?"

"A real town, with real people. Oh, it has tourists, and it has expatriates from Canada and Italy and Germany, but most of the people who live there are Dominicans."

"Does it have a beach?"

"It has a beautiful beach. And it has a few small hotels."

"Can you recommend one?"

"Sure. My baby sister manages a hotel there."

"Your baby sister? How old is she?"

"She's twenty-five. Well, she's actually a half-sister. She has a different father."

"Did she stay there when you came here?"

"No, she came here with us," Nelson said, "but she went back there after she got her degree in hotel management."

"I like the idea," Paola said. "But I have to think about it."

In the back of her mind she had been thinking about taking Briana somewhere for the spring break, which always occurred during Holy Week, but she hadn't made any definite plans. From her conversation with Nelson she knew that Danny was thinking about it. Spring break was more than three weeks away, and she had time to decide whether to include Danny, which depended on his remaining free of addictions.

When he came for dinner that Saturday she mentioned the idea while they were sitting in the kitchen after Briana had left the table and gone to her room.

"I think it would be good for Briana," he said.

"I think it would be. I want her to have an experience that gets her motivated again."

"Is she doing her homework?"

"Yeah, she is, but she's only doing it because she's supposed to. She isn't doing it because she wants to. And I don't know if she wants to do anything."

"She wants to take a vacation with us."

"I know she does, but I don't want to make plans and then disappoint her."

"I understand. I promise I won't fuck things up."

She looked at him, hoping he really meant it. "If we go together, we can't all stay in the same room. I mean, she's almost eighteen."

"I'll stay in a separate room. If I stayed in the same room as you, we'd be in violation of our agreement, wouldn't we?"

"I don't know. It says we can't live together."

"Well, maybe it doesn't apply to taking a vacation together."

"In any case," Paola told him, "we'll get two rooms, with you in one room and Briana and me in the other."

"That sounds fine."

"Nelson says you're working well."

"I like working with Nelson. I never thought I would, but I do. And I'm learning a lot from him. Maybe there's hope for me getting a license someday."

"Yeah, there's hope. It takes a while, but once you have your license you have something."

"I'm beginning to see that. I mean, from looking at Al and Nelson."

"I'm glad," she said, conscious of the fact that he was looking at her when he said that. "So I'll book the trip."

She went to the foot of the stairs and yelled up to Briana, who came down within a few minutes. She told Briana about their plan, and Briana happily came and hugged her, then happily went and hugged her father, and finally stood in front of them, jumping up and down like a cheerleader.

From then until their departure date everything went well. Briana did her homework, and Danny came to work and remained free of addictions. During that time she had another session with Janice, who supported their plan to take a vacation together and suggested that they talk with her about it, all together, after they returned. Briana had her weekly sessions, and they seemed to be helping her, but there was still something missing.

They left on a Saturday morning, on the same airline they had taken to Punta Cana, and they arrived around noon. What struck Paola when they emerged from the terminal after going through immigration and customs was the large number of people waiting for travelers. It looked like there were three to four family members for every passenger on the plane, which told her that family was important here.

With the help of the guys who surrounded them, spotting them as tourists, they got a taxi and gave the driver directions. Looking out the window, Paola saw fields of what she assumed was sugar cane, and then a town along the road with a restaurant and a food store. Evidently wanting to introduce them to the local culture, the driver played merengues from a compact disk player on his dashboard, which was graced by a statue of the Blessed Mother. She later learned that it was a statue of Our Lady of Altagracia, the patroness of the country.

The highway went through the city of Puerto Plata, where she was impressed by the activity on the streets. The driver explained in fairly good English that people were preparing for Semana Santa, which along with its solemn holy days was also a time for parties. He said that a lot of people took time off from work to attend church and have parties on the beach. He said the best beer was Presidente and the best rum was Brugal Añejo.

After turning off the highway they drove by a neighborhood of densely crowded houses, mostly wooden shacks with corrugated metal roofs. The houses were painted a spectrum of bright colors, but that didn't hide the fact that this neighborhood was a slum. And from her position between her parents in the back seat, Briana looked out the window of the car as if she was afraid that they were going to stay here.

They climbed to higher ground and came to a plaza, which had a church on one side and commercial buildings on the other sides. They had plastered facings, painted white, with terracotta roofs. From there they went up a hill and turned onto a street that ran along the ridge, from which they got their first glimpse of the sunny green ocean.

They went down the other side of the hill, and through a gate to the hotel, which as Nelson had said was close to the beach.

A young woman, conservatively dressed in a skirt and blouse, came out to greet them, saying: "I'm Yudelka, Nelson's baby sister. Welcome to Santa Cruz."

"Thank you," Paola said, shaking her hand. "I'm Paola."

"I'm Danny."

"And I'm Briana."

They both shook hands with the manager.

"I'll have the porter show you to your rooms," Yudelka said

with a noticeable Bronx accent. "You've come here at a great time. It's Semana Santa."

"The taxi driver told us," Paola said. "He said it's a time for attending church and having parties."

"Most people do both, but some people only attend church or only have parties. Whatever they do, it's okay. *No hay problema.*"

Their rooms were on the third floor, which was the top floor. There wasn't an elevator but they didn't mind climbing the stairs. Each room had a queen size bed, a cooking area, and a balcony that overlooked the ocean. Danny took one of the rooms, while Paola and Briana took the other.

When they had unpacked they got into their swimsuits and headed for the beach. It was after three now, but the sun was still warm, and it felt good as Paola strolled with her husband and her daughter onto the soft, tan sand. The beach was a crescent, maybe three miles long, with hills at both ends. It was evidently sheltered by a reef because the waves were gentle.

They slowly waded into the water, which was just the right temperature, and eventually they reached a point where they could no longer touch bottom. At that point, floating, Briana put an arm around each of her parents, saying: "This is what I dreamed of."

They had dinner at a nearby Italian restaurant, where they had pizza with sausage and mushrooms, and they spent the next morning on the beach, where they swam and walked and lay in long chairs that they rented from a guy with a Yankees cap. Around noon they returned to their rooms, showered, and dressed, and headed down the road along the beach, looking for a place to have lunch.

After a while they saw through the trees a place on the beach with chairs and tables on the sand and a blue-painted wooden building with a sign that said: "Joop's Beach Bar."

They walked to the building and saw a slate with the day's specials written in chalk. Among them was a chicken dish, and deciding to try it, they sat down at a table that overlooked the beach. A pretty girl in tight jeans came and gave them menus and took their drink orders. Paola and Danny ordered beers, and Briana ordered a Coke.

According to the menu the chicken came with rice and beans and ripe plantains, which sounded like real Dominican food, so they all ordered it. As she sipped her beer, looking out at the shimmering ocean, Paola noticed out of the corner of her eye that someone was approaching them. It was a woman, maybe a few years older than her, dressed professionally in khaki pants and a light blue top, with coffee-colored skin and dark hair in a ponytail. Around her neck was a fine gold chain, at the end of which hung a gold cross.

"Are you Americans?" the woman asked, stopping in front of them.

"Yeah," Paola said. "How did you guess?"

"I heard you guys talking, and it sounded like you had New York accents."

"I guess we do. I'm from Yonkers, and my husband's from the Bronx."

"I'm from the Bronx," the woman said. "I was born here in Santa Cruz, but my family went to America when I was five, so I grew up in the Bronx."

"Are you visiting family?"

"No, I live here. I live in the *barrio*, next to my clinic. I'm a family practitioner."

"Where did you get your medical degree?"

"At Albert Einstein in the Bronx. I got my undergraduate degree at St. Catherine in Yonkers," the woman added as if she was proud of it.

"You're kidding," Paola said. "I went to St. Catherine. I got a degree in business. What year did you graduate?"

"It was 1987, thirty years ago."

"I went there later. Would you like to join us?"

"I already had lunch, but I'll have coffee with you. My name is Daria."

"I'm Paola. This is my husband Danny, and this is our daughter

Briana. She's a senior in high school, and she's thinking about the nursing program at St. Catherine."

"That's a good program," Daria said while Danny got a chair from another table. "So you want to be a nurse?"

"I'm thinking about it," Briana said noncommittally.

"It's a great profession. I have a wonderful nurse working with me. I couldn't do anything without her."

Daria sat down and signaled to the waitress, who came and took her order in Spanish.

"What made you come back here?" Paola asked.

"I was working at a clinic in the Bronx, and I came back here to visit my relatives, and I saw there was a need, so I built a clinic." Daria smiled. "It wasn't that easy, but you don't want to hear the whole story."

"You said it's in the *barrio*. Is that the first neighborhood we saw when we drove into town?"

"Yeah, it's the poor neighborhood. It's also the most populous neighborhood. The last time we counted we had six thousand people."

"That must keep you busy."

"It does. That's why I come here every day and take a break and look at the ocean." Daria gazed out at the ocean as if it was a source of strength. And then she turned to Briana, asking: "Why do you want to be nurse?"

"I don't know if I want to be nurse, but if I do," Briana said haltingly, "it's because I want to help people."

"That's the right motivation. Have you worked in a hospital?"

"No, but I was a patient in a hospital."

"Did they help you?"

"Oh, yeah."

Daria studied her. "You know what? I think you should come and visit my clinic and see how we help people. Would you like to do that?"

Briana turned to her mother as if for an answer.

"Would you?" Paola asked her.

"Yeah, I guess."

"If you're not busy, you could come tomorrow morning. What's a good time for you?"

"Would ten in the morning work for you?" Paola asked.

"That would be perfect," Daria said. "I'll meet you at the church at ten so I can take you there. It's not easy finding your way in the *barrio*."

Daria had her coffee, and when their lunch arrived she left them to go back to work.

They took another way back to their hotel just to see more of the town, and that was how Danny happened to see the electric company doing a project to replace the old wooden poles with concrete poles. After pausing to watch a crew of men installing a new pole he told Paola he had something to do while they were visiting the clinic. With a smile she imagined him watching them install poles and connect lines, telling them in English how to do their job.

The next morning she and Briana walked to the church while Danny headed down the street where the electric crew was working. They arrived at the church before ten, and since the door was open, Paola peeked in and saw a few people kneeling in the pews, praying. Since it was Good Friday in four days, she wondered if she could get Danny and Briana to go with her to the afternoon service, even though it would be in Spanish.

She had just turned from the doorway when Daria appeared, today wearing a white top over khaki pants. Daria greeted them with a smile and asked them to go with her. She led them from the plaza into a street that turned from pavement into gravel. On both sides there were wooden houses painted blue and green and pink, with corrugated metal roofs. Alongside the street was a drainage ditch that had standing water in it. The side streets were mud, with a ditch at the side and puddles in the middle. There were no cars, but as they walked a motorbike whizzed by. There were people on the street—old women, young men, and mothers with babies. At least half of the people they passed were mothers with babies.

As they walked through the streets everyone greeted Daria, saying *"Hola, doctora,"* and *"Que Dios le bendiga, doctora. "* From the way they looked at Daria it was obvious that they loved her, and from the way she responded to them it was obvious that she loved them. It was also obvious that Daria was someone who loved her job. And Paola hoped that this woman would become a role model for her daughter.

After walking for a while they turned at a corner where there was a small grocery store in a building made of concrete blocks. In front were two chickens scratching for food, completely ignored by the light brown dog that was lying on its side about two feet away as if it was desperately in need of rest.

From there the street gradually rose, and finally at the top of the hill was the clinic in a larger building made of concrete blocks that were plastered over and painted white. Instead of the usual corrugated metal, it had a roof of terracotta. Above the door was a sign that said: "Clínica Altagracia."

"This is it," Daria said, opening the door.

They followed her into a reception room, where they were greeted by a girl in a bright yellow top seated behind a metal desk.

Daria introduced them to the girl, asked them to wait a minute and went through a door. While she was gone Paola looked around at the people who were patiently waiting to see the doctor—men and women, old and young, mothers with babies, probably wearing their better clothes for their visit to the doctor.

Daria returned with scrubs in one hand and a magazine in the other. She handed the scrubs to Briana and the magazine to Paola, saying: "For a few hours I'm going to let Briana observe what we do here. I'm sorry I don't have a more recent issue of this magazine, but it takes a while for them to get here."

"No problem," Paola said, saying in English what she had heard them say in Spanish. "I'll be fine."

Holding the scrubs, Briana followed Daria through the door.

Paola sat down in an empty plastic chair next to a woman who was holding a baby. It was hard to tell which one of them was there to see the doctor, they were both so stoical.

The magazine was a two-month-old issue of *The New Yorker*, which Paola read only in doctors' offices, so she didn't mind that it wasn't the latest. She found an article that held her interest and enabled her to pass the time, though she was always conscious of patients coming and going, sitting down and getting up when their names were called by the receptionist.

After she finished the article she stopped reading and imagined Briana observing what the nurse did to help Daria. And with her eyes on the image of Our Lady of Altagracia, which hung on the wall opposite her, she prayed that her daughter would be inspired by the experience.

When Briana returned, having shed the scrubs, there was a glow in her face that Paola hadn't seen in a long time. Daria came behind her and gently laid a hand on her shoulder as if she was performing a rite of conferral, saying: "You were great."

With an even brighter glow, Briana said: "Thanks."

Paola thanked Daria, who seemed to have known exactly what Briana needed, and they were led out of the *barrio* by a young man who evidently did odd jobs at the clinic. Not wanting to break the spell, Paola didn't say anything until they were back at the plaza, where she thanked the young man and watched him go.

She faced Briana, about to say: "Well?"

Before she could say it Briana said: "I want to be a nurse."

They hugged each other as if they had been separated for a long, long time.

That night after Briana had gone to bed, exhausted from her day at the clinic, Paola and Danny were sitting on the balcony of her room, sipping wine. It was a perfect night with only a few clouds in the sky, and without any moon or any urban light pollution they could see a lot of stars. In the gentle breeze from the ocean they could smell salt.

They had talked about their daughter's resolution to be a nurse, and it led to Danny saying: "So she knows what she wants to be, and I know what I want to be."

Paola waited for him to continue.

"I want to be a good husband, a good father, and a good worker. If I can be all those things, I'll be happy."

"Are you sure?"

"I'm sure."

Her mind still had doubts, but her heart had faith. "So we'll end our separation agreement, and we'll renew our wedding vows."

"At St. Brigid's?"

"Yeah. At St. Brigid's."

Without another word her right hand and his left hand found each other and clasped each other, confirming their intent.

BOOK CLUB GUIDE

The Lineman

Tom Milton

Introduction

Paola is the youngest of three children, with two older brothers, and when they both decide to pursue professional careers her father entrusts her with Borgatti Electric, the business he founded as a young man and built over a lifetime of hard work. As a girl, Paola doesn't want to be a teacher or a nurse or a secretary or a flight attendant, the approved careers for females at the time. She wants to be an electrician, and instead of going to college she becomes an apprentice at her father's business and works her way through the long process of getting her license.

While in this process she goes to a bar with her friend Gabby for their first legal drink, and there she meets Danny, a lineman for the electric company. Paola and Danny are immediately attracted to each other, and they begin dating, first in a foursome with Gabby and Danny's roommate Ron, and then as a couple. Their relationship develops, and after two years they get married. For a while they live in his apartment, and then after Paola gets pregnant they buy a house near the two-family house where her parents live. The baby arrives, but its delivery is so difficult that Paola is told not to risk another pregnancy. They are grateful for having at least one child, whom they name Briana, and for sixteen years they live happily, raising their daughter and doing their jobs.

Then everything changes when Danny, still working as a lineman, falls from a cherry picker onto the pavement and crushes his shoulder. After two major surgeries, and months of pain and physical therapy, he hopes that the company will let him resume working as a lineman, which is more than just a job for him—it's his identity as a man. So when the company decides he's no longer physically able to work as a lineman and instead offers him a job managing work crews, he refuses to accept their decision and sues them for making him work with faulty equipment. When he loses his lawsuit for justifiable reasons, he loses his job and he loses the compensation that the company has been paying him for his injury, so he must find other employment. Paola, whose father has by now given her full ownership of Borgatti Electric, offers Danny a job as an electrician and an equal partnership in the business. He tries this job, and he does it well, but he doesn't love it the way he loved his job as a lineman, and unable to deal with the new reality, he gets addicted to a series of things from opioids to video games to online gambling.

He becomes addicted to opioids during the months when he has surgeries to repair the damage from his fall, including a shoulder replacement. To manage the pain, he continues taking opioids after his doctor stops prescribing them, which he acquires in the gray market. When his condition begins to interfere with his ability to do his job as an electrician, Paola realizes that he's addicted to opioids, and she gets him into a treatment program, which helps him become drug free. But it isn't long before he gets into video games, which he plays on his computer in the basement after dinner. Briana joins him, presumably after she has completed her homework. She is now a junior in high school, a good student whose grades are important because she wants to get into the nursing program at St. Catherine College, so Paola wants to be sure that Briana isn't cutting short her homework to play video games. When Paola goes down to the basement and sees that they are playing violent games, whose object is to kill as many people as possible on the enemy side, she forbids Briana from playing them, and she asks Danny to find games that are nonviolent. By then she realizes that he's addicted to video games, and she gets him into a treatment program that helps him overcome this addiction.

While playing nonviolent games, including card games like hearts and gin rummy, Danny and Briana discover online poker, which he starts playing after Briana has gone upstairs to bed. For a while he wins, but inevitably he starts losing, and in trying to make up his losses he keeps playing, and he keeps losing, until he has amassed an enormous debt, which he owes to the organization that runs the gambling. When he can't pay it, the organization threatens to hurt his daughter unless he finds a way to pay it, and Danny abuses his power as a full partner in Borgatti Electric to take a loan on behalf of the business from a bank with a dubious reputation. Since he has authority to borrow on his sole signature, Paola is unaware of the loan until the bank sends an invoice for the first instalment. Meanwhile, Danny has continued gambling, hoping to win enough to pay off the loan before Paola finds out about it, but he has been losing, and he now has another debt to the organization.

With the help of her brother Dominic, an accountant who helps small businesses manage their finances, Paola learns that their business isn't capable of repaying the bank loan. Their only major asset is the building that her father worked a lifetime to acquire. Conscious of his having entrusted her with the business, Paola rules out taking a mortgage on the building to repay the bank loan. She asks her other brother Anthony, a lawyer, to examine the loan documents to see if for some reason they might be invalid, and the only possibility is a clause in the partnership agreement stating that if Danny becomes incapacitated, then his powers are terminated, but this is a long shot. He refers Paola to a litigation lawyer who pursues the possibility that in making a loan that couldn't be repaid, the bank failed to do due diligence, but this is also a long shot. While waiting for the results of these two actions, Paola explores the possibility of increasing the mortgage on their home, and she meets with a realtor and with her bank to see if that will generate enough money to pay down the bank loan and to pay off the additional debt to the organization. When that doesn't work, her last resort is to sell their house.

Though she knew that this would be hard on Briana, she hoped that by moving into the two-family home owned by her parents she could keep her family together, but Danny becomes addicted to opioids again, and he begins to run up a debt to pay for his habit. With no more resources, Paola is facing financial ruin. She has taken away his power to borrow on behalf of the business as well as his ownership position, but as his wife she's personally liable for his debts. Since she still loves Danny and still has hope for their marriage, she doesn't divorce him, but she arranges a legal separation so that she won't be liable for his debts. The only condition is that they have to live separately, and while Danny seems able to deal with this, Briana refuses to deal with it. And she's now on a course that began with rebellion and could end in self-destruction.

A conversation with Tom Milton

I noticed that your last two novels have a similar subject. They're both about men who lose their identities as a result of losing their jobs.

With the changes in our economy, it's a major issue. A lot of men have lost jobs that gave them identities, and feeling they have no place in the world, they can be attracted to extremist movements or they can get addicted to things.

In this novel the story is told from the point of view of the woman who tries to help the man. It's not told from his point of view. Why not?

Because I'm interested in the challenges that the woman faces in trying to help him. And that's not new in my approach. My first published novel, *No Way to Peace*, was about women trying to help men deal with the war in Argentina.

I noticed this situation in your other novels. For example, A Shower of Roses *was about a woman trying to save a government agent from self-destruction, and* Invisible Wounds *was about a woman trying to help a veteran with PTSD.*

As I said, I'm interested in the challenges that the women face in trying to help men with serious problems.

Do you think this is a common situation?

I think it's fairly common, though there's also the opposite situation. The women have problems, and the men try to help them. But I'm more interested in the former situation, so that's what I usually write about.

In all your novels you present strong female characters. They have values that they try to live by, and when they make commitments they keep them. What's your purpose in doing this?

I believe that fiction should show not only the trials of being human but also the triumphs. For all the terrible things we're doing in the world today, I still have a positive view of humanity, and I want to show my readers positive role models.

Your heroines have a variety of occupations. I can think of a social worker, a journalist, a teacher, a civil rights activist, a singer, a detective, a nurse, an athlete, a fund raiser, a physician, a goat farmer, a printing manager, a therapist, a nun, and others. And in this novel your heroine is an electrician, the manager of a small business.

I want to show how anyone can be a heroine, no matter what they do for a living.

They also have a variety of ethnic backgrounds, including Irish, Polish, Italian, Spanish, Mexican, Dominican, and Puerto Rican.

I want to show the universality of the qualities that make them heroines.

Are your heroines based on people you've known?

In a way they are. I mean, I don't base my characters on my family, friends, colleagues, acquaintances, or students, but I use their characteristics, and I use their situations.

Would I recognize any of these people?

I don't think so. In my early novels, which luckily were never published, when there was a mother in the situation, my mother always thought it was her. Of course it wasn't, but she always thought it was.

What about your wife?

Oh, she's in all my novels, at least some aspect of her.

Let's get back to this novel. I notice that after Danny loses his job and sees that he's been replaced by a Puerto Rican, he blames the company policy of promoting diversity, displaying an attitude of racism that his wife has never seen before. And in The Last Resort *after Karl loses his job, he joins a white nationalist movement that blames nonwhite immigrants for our country's problems. They both resort to racism.*

We can see this happening among white males who have lost jobs that they expected to have for their lifetimes, jobs that gave them identities.

But they weren't racist before they lost their jobs.

They didn't show it. Danny never paid attention to Puerto Ricans, and Karl never knew a nonwhite immigrant, but racism was latent in them, and it was stirred up by their loss of identity.

So racism gives them a new identity?

It gives them an easy identity as white males, as members of the dominant group.

That explains why Danny has trouble working for Nelson, a nonwhite Dominican. But eventually he likes working for Nelson, so something good can happen in these situations.

I know it can, or I wouldn't show it happening.

Now, let's talk about Danny's addictions. Through your characters you offer some explanations of why Danny keeps getting addicted. The simple explanation is his inability to deal with his new situation.

From what I've seen and heard and read, that could be the explanation in a lot of cases. If you're in a situation that you can't deal with, then one apparent solution is to escape from it by getting addicted to something. Of course, that's not a real solution. It only puts you in a worse situation.

I think it's a good explanation. But you offer another explanation through the ex-nun who's now a therapist. It's not caring about yourself.

That's the idea I started with, the deadly sin of *acedia,* which we usually call sloth though it's not simply being lazy. As the ex-nun says, it's a darkness of the soul, an indifference to God. And if you're in that state of mind, you don't care about yourself.

Danny acts as if he doesn't care about himself, but his daughter thinks he cares about her and her mother, so he has a conflict, which he escapes through his addictions.

His daughter could be right, and his caring about her and her mother could be his saving grace.

So if the problem is not caring about yourself, then the solution might be to care enough about others so you care about yourself for their sake. But that's not something you can do with drug therapy.

Drug therapy can help you deal with the physiological effects of addiction, but drugs only deal with the symptoms of the problem. To deal with the cause of the problem, you need another kind of therapy. You need a change of heart.

Well, I won't spoil the ending. I'll just say that my heart goes out to Paola, and to your other heroines who try to help men with their problems.

That's why I write, to make your heart go out to them.

Discussion questions

1. How was Danny affected by losing his job as a lineman with the electric company?

2. Why did Danny have trouble accepting the job of managing work crews?

3. What finally turned Danny against the company?

4. Did it help Danny for his coworker Joe to cover up what really happened in the cherry picker?

5. If Danny had consciously lied about what happened in the cherry picker, would that have changed Paola's relationship with him?

6. Describe Paola's relationship with her father. How was it similar to Danny's relationship with his father? How was it different?

7. Should Paola have given Danny a partnership in the business with equal powers?

8. Why did Danny get addicted to opioids, video games, and gambling?

9. Did Paola fail in any way in her efforts to help Danny with his addictions?

10. Unlike many addicts, Danny was able to overcome his addictions at least periodically. Explain what might have motivated him.

11. Why was Paola unwilling to take a mortgage on the building owned by the family business?

12. Did Paola do the right thing in arranging a legal separation from Danny?

13. What obstacles did Paola face in her relationship with Briana?

14. Did Janice provide a useful insight in telling Paola about the deadly sin of *acedia*?

15. What finally stirred Briana out of her lethargy?

16. How did Briana's decision to be a nurse help her parents get together again?